THE CAPTAIN
MUST DIE

Other books by Robert Colby

Fiction

Beautiful but Bad
Executive Wife
The California Crime Book
The Faster She Runs
Make Mine Vengeance
Murder Times Five
Run for the Money
Secret of the Second Door
The Star Trap
These Lonely, These Dead

THE CAPTAIN
MUST DIE
ROBERT COLBY

PROLOGUE BOOKS

F+W Media, Inc.

Published in electronic format by
PROLOGUE BOOKS
an imprint of F+W Media, Inc.
10151 Carver Road
Blue Ash, Ohio 45242
www.prologuebooks.com

eISBN 10: 1-4405-3732-1
eISBN 13: 978-1-4405-3732-5

POD ISBN 10: 1-4405-5799-3
POD ISBN 13: 978-1-4405-5799-6

This is a work of fiction. Names, characters, corporations, institutions, organizations, events, or locales in this novel are either the product of the author's imagination or, if real, used fictitiously. The resemblance of any character to actual persons (living or dead) is entirely coincidental.

This work has been previously published in print format by:
Fawcett Publications, Inc., New York, NY.

For Francesca
And for Roger, Paul, and Nona Crossman

Chapter One

*T*he train had barely come to a stop at the Union Station in Louisville, when the tall man with the flimsy black suitcase shouldered the conductor out of the way and jumped to the platform.

". . . hell's the matter with you!" the conductor called after him. But, though he heard clearly, the tall man didn't look back. The anger in him was too large a thing, too deeply banked to permit of small irritations. The thing inside him was quiet and intent, having the power of long development, like a storm that gathers force in the secret wastes of the ocean and moves stealthily inland for destruction.

The tall man had a loose-jointed and awkward physical power about him as he moved with long strides through the waiting room of the depot. His long, high-cheekboned face ended in a narrow jut of jaw. He had a thin straight nose, a wide mouth, and sullen brown eyes. It was a face that at twenty-six had been facile with teasing humor and boyish pleasantness. Now, at thirty-eight, it was a face drawn together with shrewd watchfulness and contempt.

The tall man was not aware that the frayed, black suitcase was heavy. He swung it along with him like a child's toy, the bony knuckles of one great hand jutting from the handle like the knobs of railroad spikes.

He set the case down by a cab outside the station. When the driver had placed it in the trunk, he ducked his angular body inside the cab and sank onto a corner of the seat, smoothing the trousers of his rumpled chocolate gabardine. He gave an address off South Third and the hack pulled away sharply.

"You picked a hot one," said the driver over his shoulder.

"What?"

"Hot day to land here," the driver said.

"Oh," said the tall man. "Yeah. Plenty hot." His voice was flat and remote as though his thoughts were pulled from a difficult problem. He had not noticed that it was hot; was hardly conscious of the drab buildings of the city he had never before seen.

"Bad summer," the driver said. "Worse that fifty-four. Me, I'll take San Fran anytime. Gonna take the missus and head out there soon as we save a few bucks. Never did like this town. Dull as it's hot. Excuse me, mister. You come from around here?"

"What?"

"This your home? I mean, no offense —"

"Listen, bud," the tall man said. "Why don't you wheel this wreck and just shut up. You got troubles? I'll punch your card for you."

"Sorry, George," the driver said. "Didn't know you was touchy about the home town."

"Just shut up," the tall man said again without anger. The driver mumbled something but the tall man wasn't listening. He was wondering now if he should have called from the station; if Barney had arrived from Los Angeles the night before with the cunning, evil box; if Cal, who had taken the apartment a week ago, was waiting there for him as planned. Or was he in the booth of some dark bar, squeezed against a tight curve of some sweatered yokel he had picked up the first night in from Denver. Cal was always the operator.

Well, that kind of stuff would have to wait till later. For a thing like this, you needed a certain discipline or it would fall apart. Well, they were all acquainted with discipline. And he was going to enforce it. He was going to hold the purpose together. He was going to keep reminding, keep lighting the fire. God! It shouldn't be necessary. Who could forget! Not Barney. Never. And not Cal, really. You just had to keep him in line. And he would have certain special uses. They would be able to use that handsome pan of his. And all of his operating tricks would help twist the knife.

The cab ground tires against the curb and came to a halt. "This is it," the driver said. "Twenty-three seventy you said?"

"Yeah. Right." The tall man leaned out the window, studying a tree-storied apartment building that joined other buildings like it and seemed to stretch endlessly away in monotonous repetition.

The tall man paid the driver the exact amount of the fare, lifted the suitcase from the sidewalk, and moved briskly toward the entrance of twenty-three seventy as the cab departed with an angry grinding of gears.

In the vestibule, he paused long enough to study the mail boxes. Then with a grunt he hoisted himself and the case up three flights to apartment 3C, rang the bell.

The door was opened by a deep-chested, heavy-shouldered man with straight black hair. He had small but strongly handsome features, bright, clever eyes, coolly green, full of amusement. He was a head shorter than the tall man.

"Cal," the tall man said. "Thought you'd be out

boozing with some doll."

"In the afternoon, Brick?" said the one called Cal. "Too hot and too early."

Brick, the tall one, gave him a look and pushed past into the living room, glancing disinterestedly at the twenty-by-fifteen space with its anonymous clutter of maple pieces, setting the suitcase on the oval throw rug. "Where's Barney?" he said.

"Kitchen," said Cal. "Saw you coming. He's building a cool one."

Brick bent himself onto the sofa. "Lousy trip," he said. "Hate trains. Had to sit up all night. Everything set?"

"What's to set?" Cal said. "Waiting for you. My God, but you still look pale."

"After twelve years, you don't get colored up in a couple of weeks," said Brick disgustedly. "Plenty of time for that."

"Yeah. We'll really live!" Cal said, dropping into a chair.

Brick gave him a sharp glance. "Don't be in any hurry, hear? Don't screw this up now. Do I have to keep reminding . . ."

"Hey! Brick! Welcome home. Brought you one for a dusty throat."

The man who stood in the doorway of the kitchen was medium-sized and stocky. His hair was the color of new rope and began far back from his forehead. He had bearlike shoulders. A thick neck and powerful biceps. His features were blunt, his eyes flat blue. He carried a trio of drinks in the palm of one hand. He set the drinks on the coffee table in front of the tall man and extended his hand.

"How was New York?" he said. "You tie on a big one, Brick?"

Brick smiled, took the extended hand without rising. "Same old rabbit hutch," he said. "Everyone on the jump for lettuce. Nah, I took it easy. Nothin' there for me anymore."

"Thought you would've found a live one," said Cal, picking up one of the drinks.

"That's your department," said Brick, lighting a cigarette and squinting over the flame of his lighter. "I had other things on my mind. How about you? You been here a week. You check the setup?"

"Sure," said Cal. "I've got a whole notebook full of items. I could tell you what time he goes to bed and what kind of tooth paste he uses."

"Good! Don't suppose you checked his wife?" Brick said wryly.

"You kidding? I could tell you what size —"

"Forget it. I was sure you didn't miss anything there."

"She hasn't changed," said Cal. "Just filled out a bit — in all the right places. That's one part of the deal I like." ·

"You better like all of it," said Brick. He picked up his highball and twisted it in his hand.

"I like all of it," said Cal. "All but the way it ends. I don't know about that."

The tall man was very still for a moment. "You better get to like that, too," he said quietly. "You better live with it, get the feel of it. You got a short memory."

Cal was silent.

"What about you, Barney?" said Brick. "You like the end?"

"I can almost taste it," said Barney. "The end should come first."

"Oh, no," said Brick. "That's where you're wrong. A thing like this should build. It should begin slowly, in a very small way. First it heckles, you see. Irritates like a boil. Then it tightens." The tall man slowly brought his fingers together until they clenched into a knotty fist. "And when it tightens, it frightens. You see? You got to have the fear first. That's really the best part. That's the part you drag out, like you were sipping a good wine. Then you back up the fear and it gets serious. It begins to crush and crush until it splinters like match wood and breaks apart. You see? Then! That's the time . . . The end is almost an anti-climax. Because twelve years is a long time. A very long time. Right, Cal?"

"That's right," said Cal.

"Barney?"

"A hell of a long time."

Brick washed his mouth with the last gulp and swallowed. He looked around the room. "What's the deal on the apartment, Cal?"

"I took it for a month. But we can have it as long as we need. Two bedrooms," he jerked a thumb over his shoulder. "At ninety-five per."

Brick nodded.

"What's in the suitcase?" asked Barney, leaning forward. He winked. "Besides the laundry, I mean."

Brick set his glass on the table, unfolded himself from the couch, crossed to the center of the room, and laid the suitcase on its side. Squatting, he opened it, shoving aside clothing, digging to the bottom, coming up with three stubby .38 revolvers. "All new," he said. "All alike." He passed out two and dropped the other back into the case.

"Nice," said Cal. "Very nice." He broke the gun and twirled the cylinder.

"Pretty toy," said Barney, weighing his in his hand. "Real belly-jammer. But give me the old forty-five for serious trouble."

"For a real friend, I'll take this one," said Brick. From the bottom of the case he produced a shiny rifle in two sections, fitting it together, then squinting across the room through the telescopic sight. "Thirty-o-six," he said. "Neat as a razor. No guesswork." He cocked the rifle and squeezed the trigger. There was the thin snap of the hammer falling.

"What's that one for?" said Cal.

"You'll see," said Brick. "You'll see." He dismantled the rifle and put it away in the bottom of the suitcase. He held out his hand. "I'll take the rest of the iron, too," he said. "This part comes later. Until then, we go out clean." He took the revolvers and tucked them away.

"When do we start?" said Barney with a note of excitement.

Brick looked at his watch. "Two-thirty now," he said. "What time does he fold, Cal?"

"Somewhere between five and five-fifteen. Usually right around five sharp."

The tall man stood up and looked down at the other two. A muscle worked in his jaw. "Then that's when it starts," he said. "At five o'clock sharp."

Chapter Two

At ten minutes before five o'clock on Wednesday afternoon, Gregory Driscoll sat in his private office at radio and television station WGDE — the G-D-E of the call letters standing for Gregory Driscoll Enterprises. Located in the heart of Louisville, it was one of the largest stations in the city. But it was only one of several Driscoll holdings. There was the Driscoll Land Development Company, the Driscoll Drive-in Theaters and the Gregstop Suburban Hotel. Gregory Driscoll was a man who believed in the security of multiple investment.

He was a young forty-three. At twenty-four, when his grandfather, the millionaire owner of an immense dairy, had left him a hundred and fifty thousand dollars, he had bought the failing radio station for ninety-five thousand. The station was small and hungry, but he had slowly brought it back to life and prestige. Later he had added television and signed a contract with one of the big networks to become their Louisville outlet. The station then became a gold mine and he had used the same technique in other ventures — buying nearly bankrupt businesses and rebuilding them with his peculiar talent for organization.

He was slightly over middle height, with gray-peppered black hair and bushy eyebrows, a strong nose and chin, a firm mouth and intense gray eyes. He was not given to wasted motion and seemed a man in constant repose. But he was tightly put together and there was something coiled about him. Like a smooth machine idling, he looked ready to spring forward at the press of some secret button. This was partly due to his wiry build, but mostly because of that latent intensity in his eyes. He was a man who listened with such unblinking attention and immobility that the speaker often found himself a little awkward, a little groping for words. However formidable he appeared, he could be charming and witty when the conversation was of small importance.

He spent most of his time in the office of the station, using it as a capitol and liking it most because it was the seat of his early success.

Now, at ten minutes to five, he signed the last of the payroll checks for the following day's disbursement and began to straighten his desk. He was a man of tidy habits and never left before the desk was clean of that day's business. He spent the next several minutes consulting a notebook, transcribing from it to his desk pad Thursday's appointments and duties.

At one minute to five, he entered the small bathroom adjoining his once, removed tooth paste and brush from a cabinet and brushed his teeth assiduously, rinsing his mouth with a wash. He scrubbed and dried his hands, inspecting his fingernails minutely. Glancing in the mirror, he gave his tie a small, centering wrench, then opened a closet and removed a gray fedora, placing it carefully on his head, giving the brim a downward twist. Passing his desk, he picked up the signed checks and laid them on his secretary's desk, said goodnight pleasantly and was gone. It was three minutes after five.

Outside, he crossed the street to the private parking lot used by the station employees. He backed his dark blue fifty-seven Buick sedan from the space that bore his name and rolled out onto the street, heading east in the five o'clock traffic. He twisted the knob of the dashboard radio and began to listen attentively to the remainder of the five o'clock news delivered by a WGDE announcer. He made note that the announcer had mispronounced the name of a local official and that he must speak to his radio program director about it. It was the third of such local mispronouncements during that week, but he would not make an issue of the matter. The man was new and should be given a reasonable time to acquaint himself with the sometimes difficult names of Louisville VIPs. He would have the newsroom place in phonetics all unusual names.

It was shortly after he crossed Market Street and accelerated from a right turn that he noticed above the radio announcer's cadence, a slight clacking sound somewhat like that made by a sticky valve. He switched off the radio, pushed down on the accelerator and listened. There it was again! At almost the same moment his eye caught the warning of the oil indicator that he had lost pressure. And now he began to notice a burning odor, like overheated brakes. He pulled in at the next service station.

"Check my oil, will you please?" he said to the attendant. The man lifted the hood and meanwhile, Driscoll went around the car feeling his tires. They were almost too hot to touch. He joined the man eying his oil stick.

"Tried it twice," the man said. "Not a drop."

Driscoll tried it himself and got the same result. "Strange," he said. "Just changed the oil the other day."

"Maybe they drained it but forgot to refill it," said the attendant.

Driscoll shook his head. "I doubt it. Pressure was

all right this morning."

"Damn funny," said the man. "Shall I put it on the rack?"

"Please. And while you've got it up there, have a look at my brakes. They seem to be overheating."

"Yes, sir. But you'll have to wait a moment. Grease job just finishing up."

"I'll wait," he said, and began to wander absently around the station. He felt now the first edge of irritation. It was disgustingly hot and at home in the air-conditioned den where there was a small bar, his wife Madge would be mixing Martinis. Madge had a talent for Martinis. He could taste the dry, bittersweetness of the first sip, feel the cool air of the conditioner. And there was always the surge of anticipation at seeing Madge after the day. She was the one holding he had not completely possessed for a long time, and she produced in him an uneasy excitement. It was, in a sense, the same kind of feeling he had in closing a deal that was risky, that might not jell.

He decided against calling her. It would be only a few minutes. But in the end, they were a long time getting his car on the rack, after which there were delays as the man attended to other customers at the busy pumps, and it took the better part of an hour.

When the car was on the rack, he waited while it was hoisted, then went under with the attendant to look.

"Here's your trouble," the attendant said immediately. "Oil plug is missing."

"Missing!"

"Yup."

"How could that happen?"

"Guy who changed your oil forgot to tighten it. Worked loose and dropped out. Dumped all the oil. Another few miles and you'd have burned her out."

"Well, they'll hear from me! Put in five quarts and a new plug. Hurry, please. I want to get rolling."

"Don't know if I can."

"Can what? Hurry? My God, you —"

"Don't know if I can fix it."

"Why not?"

"Don't have a plug to fit it. Have to pick it up from Buick. Closed now."

"Damn! What about the brakes?"

"I'll check."

The attendant made a circuit of the wheels. He was unable to spin any of them. "Brakes are too tight," he said. "Practically frozen solid. About to burn up. Jerk who fixed 'em didn't know what he was doing."

"Never mind," said Driscoll impatiently. "Just loosen them up and send for the plug. I'll have someone pick up the car in the morning. Now show me the phone."

He called Madge and then a taxi. It took the cab ten or fifteen minutes, but he finally got underway. By the time he arrived home, much of his good spirit had left him. Something had gone out of the day — that flow of harmony, that smooth pace of controlled living, had deserted him. He was not a man to whom little misfortunes happened with any frequency. He despised any situation over which he had no command. And this was a very odd thing. Oil plugs did not just drop from cars. Not from his cars. And no one had touched his brakes but the experts of the Buick service department.

As he went up the walk to the two-storied, English manor-type house, some oblique awareness nudged him. Something was strangely out of shape. Something about the Buick. Something beyond mere bad luck.

"What a messy thing to happen," said Madge. They were in the den and she was pouring a Martini from a full shaker into a long-stemmed glass. "Mechanical things escape me altogether," she said. "They're almost as obstinate as people." She poured the Martini into the frosty glass until it was a fraction from the top, brought it over to where Driscoll was seated, studying her.

In high heels she was almost as tall as he was. She had blueblack hair done in a shortened pageboy. She had elongated, wing shaped eyebrows. Her face was a large, unblemished oval. She had a small, ski-slide nose, a wide mouth with a thick bumper of lower lip. Her eyes had long lashes, were nearly almond-shaped and blue-green. They had a slightly disdainful look, as though they were yet to be surprised. It was an intelligent face, but slyly dominating. The figure was a gem for those who like their fruit not too forbidden and abundant with ripeness. She was thirty-four.

Driscoll sipped the drink and let it run its warm course. He felt the flush of heat leaving him under the air conditioning. There was Madge and the drink, and altogether he felt better. Relaxed. He decided to make light of the thing with the Buick. "I'll use the Thunderbird in the morning," he said. "When the Buick's delivered, I'll send it back to you."

"Lucky we have two cars," she said, pouring her own drink, standing with one knee slightly bent, in an attitude that showed the long swing of leg and thigh.

"A man should have two of everything," said Driscoll. He smiled. "Except wives put together like you."

"Sure," said Madge, "because how could you ever handle two like me?"

Driscoll considered. "I'm not even sure I can handle *one* like you." He grinned. But nevertheless he meant it.

She carried her drink to a chair facing him and dropped into it. "It's good for you to have at least one thing that's hard to handle, Greg," she said with a twist of her lips. "You need to be challenged."

"True," he said. "People should be just difficult enough not to be boring."

"Am I difficult, darling?"

"I've been trying to decide in what way for a long time. Anything remarkable happen with you today?"

"A letter from Bobby." She smiled. "Cute but not remarkable."

"Cute is about all you can ask of a ten-year-old. How's camp?"

"Well," she said, "we're doing a lot of swimming and we caught a whole mess of fish. We won a tennis tournament, and oh, yes, we like riding so much we want a pony of our own."

"We'll have to wait a bit for the pony," said Driscoll. "We get things so easily from Daddy we have a fairytale impression of life. I'm glad about the tennis. It's good to compete and win."

"I miss the little rascal," she said. "But it's a kind of vacation for me."

"Sure. Sure it is. You chase him all day in the summer and I get his best, worn-out self at night."

"Darling," she said. "Apropos of nothing, except that I just remembered, you didn't order the gas and lights turned off, did you?"

"Did I what!"

"That was only a way of leading into a strange little item," she said. "The gas and electricity were turned off today. It was, and still is, an awful mess. The refrigerator went off, all the clocks stopped, Jessie couldn't do any ironing or use any of the appliances. And on top of that, we simply stewed for a while because the air-conditioning went off, too. I was positive you wouldn't have a reason in the world to have anything turned off, but . . . ."

"Of course not! Why didn't you call me?"

"I never call you about anything I can straighten out myself."

"I appreciate that. But what happened?"

"I phoned gas and electric and they said you had ordered both turned off because we were going on vacation. So I told them there must be some mistake. They finally got the electricity on, but the gas man hasn't come yet — if he's coming at all today. Supper will be mostly cold cuts."

"Damn it to hell! Is this someone's idea of a practical joke?"

"Somehow, I don't think you're the kind people play jokes on, Greg."

"Is that a compliment?"

"Yes. In a way."

"Well, the gas and electric company shouldn't turn anything off without written authorization. Why, just anyone can pick up the phone and . . ." He was thinking now about the Buick. Maybe it was coincidence. But at that moment he felt the first probe of uneasiness.

"What time did this little episode take place?" he said casually.

"It was going on five o'clock. Why?"

"Just wondering."

"Supper's on the table, Miz Driscoll." A squat colored maid of generous proportions stood in the doorway.

"All right, Jessie," said Madge. "Soon as we finish our drinks. Not much danger of anything getting cold."

*A*t eleven-thirty, they were upstairs in the big front bedroom of their most intimate hours. Madge was slowly peeling off her clothes, oblivious to his hungry stare. It was a ritual of which he never tired. This was partly because she had a figure so rich and blatantly sensual, each unveiling was like the first. And partly because she withheld from him some secret corner of her mentality and in that sense, he went to bed every night with an exciting stranger.

"Madge?" he said now. "Are you happy?"

She stood in profile, twisting her brassiere back to front, her long fingers working on the snaps. The fingers stopped. She swung her head sideways to face him. "Of course, darling," she said, sounding a trifle annoyed. Her arched eyebrows seemed about to take flight. "You're always asking that. Shouldn't I be?" She let the brassiere fall away, dropping it to a chair. Her breasts dipped gently, rose sharply in white shimmering crests.

There was a startled moment of silence as he watched her come slowly around and reach for her garter belt. "I mean," he said, "are you happy with me?"

"Now isn't that absurd! After all these years." She didn't smile. Her face seemed to close as she withdrew into that secret place where she hid from him. "I wish you wouldn't keep asking me that. It's like you were trying to plant doubts." She smoothed a pale blue diaphanous nightgown over her body, sat down at her dressing tale and began to put up her hair with a concentration that seemed to exclude him.

"Now you've left me," he said.

"Sometimes you talk in riddles," she said with a weary detachment.

"Sometimes you pretend not to understand," he said. "And sometimes I can't find you in that polar region where you live."

"Oh, my God! Will you please stop looking for some hidden meaning in every word and every little silence and get undressed?"

"I'm sorry," he said. "And it's too intangible to

explain. It's just that I can't reach you at times.''

She dropped her hands from her hair and looked at him steadily in they mirror. ''Don't try so hard and you may have better luck. You control so many things, now you want to control thought.'' She went back to pinning her hair.

He went into the bathroom and began to run water into the tub. He felt suddenly lonely and ineffectual.

She was in bed when he came back to her, facing the wall. He opened the windows, turned out the light and crawled in next to her. When he reached for her shoulder to bring her toward him, he expected she would be rigid. But with a sigh, she rolled over and pressed against him. When he kissed her, her mouth slowly widened over his. ''I demand too much of you,'' he murmured. ''I'm sorry.''

''Don't be sorry,'' she breathed. ''You, don't demand too much. I must be selfish because I only have so much to give. Don't try to understand what I don't understand myself.'' She slid the straps of her gown over her shoulders, withdrew her arms and uncovered herself to the waist. ''Isn't this enough?''

He lay his head against her, breast. ''Yes,'' he said. ''It's enough.'' But he knew it wasn't. His life apart from her was a masterpiece of discipline and control. He sat on top of his orbit alone. People expected precise decisions and masterful judgments. And he gave them. They leaned on his strength and offered none in return. You climbed to a pinnacle and the view was glorious. But unshared. He wanted someplace where the small weaknesses in him could be exposed, left unguarded and at rest.

Madge was somehow not restful. She continued

rather than eased the tensions of the day. She called for something in him to be still alert and watchful. She was crisp and exciting and not altogether known. But she lacked a certain mothering quality, that soft comforting which takes the naked self, accepts and soothes it with uncritical love. Strange, you could lie on her soft breast and still not relax.

He made love to her and she fell asleep immediately. But he lay restless, a long time unable to quiet his thoughts. He tried to solidify something about Madge that made him uncertain of her, even a little fearful of losing her. So much so that he never burdened her with any of his deeper problems or doubts.

It hadn't always been that way. He hadn't always been uncertain of her. There had been a time more than ten years ago when he was as certain of her as his own success. A time when be knew, or thought he knew, every corner and crevice of her mind, knew her thoughts even before they formed the words that tumbled from her mouth.

They had been married a few short years then. It was after Pearl Harbor and the country was well into the war. He was involved and deeply serious about his part. Too serious. Too inflexible in his views. But she had moved with him from camp to camp and, though the war had interrupted his career, never their closeness.

She teased him about his over-developed sense of duty, his fever of patriotism, his rigidity, calling him a zealot, then picking up the army lingo, "Old by-the-numbers Driscoll, he counts cadence when we go to bed."

There was no sarcasm in her kidding, just fun. She had a wry good humor. In those days she was really intensely loyal and so companionable and necessary that he wondered how he had pushed for himself through the blank years without her.

She was restful then. Quiet and tender. Or, in good times, silly and gay.

And in those days, love-making was combustible. Spontaneous combustion. It caught fire in odd places and at ridiculous times. Not before sleep, planned and mechanical, spaced and grudging.

And then, like walking from warm bed into cold night, she betrayed him in the most disgusting, unbelievable way. He found out in secret and when she never told him, he kept the secret. Not because he wanted to. But because another thing happened that made it impossible for him to ever admit that he knew.

This was a thing of his doing, a thing he regretted long too late. Regretted not so much the act as the possibility of bias judgment which caused it.

But he despised Madge only briefly. Because he couldn't exist without her, he came to love her again. And finally to show his love.

You would have thought that with her guilty knowledge she would respond to that love. Especially long after. But no, she was never quite the same.

Nothing tangible. Nothing easy to pin down. On the surface everything was quite normal. Even many of the same words of love. But the undercurrent of feeling behind them was gone.

You couldn't talk to her. He tried. You couldn't talk around the iceberg that lay between them. You couldn't talk about something you weren't supposed to know. So, in the end, he felt cast adrift from her and, in his loneliness, turned his attention to another kind of security — the accumulation of money and holdings.

In fact, his separateness from Madge had only enforced the peculiar driving need he had to pile up money. Even when, by some standards, he was already rich. For as a boy and throughout his early manhood, be had known such devastating poverty that be had resolved to build a high, green wall against the pigsty living and shameless groveling for a dollar that had degraded him, helped to destroy his father and make a shabby drudge of his mother. So intense was the impression this poverty left upon him, he mistrusted even the banks. They had failed. And they could again. So that the largest share of his growing wealth, he kept in a secret place — never far from his reach. Yet, had Madge given him the key to *her* secret placewhere she stored the love he needed — the compulsion to hoard might soon have left him.

But she didn't. Instead she grew more and more restless. And if she wasn't unfaithful, she began to bang around the edge of infidelity. Nothing he could nail down. But widening the breach.

It wasn't just the way men reacted to her. All men reacted to a beautiful woman, married or single. It must be the way she reacted to them.

At one of those roving, loose scrambles called cocktail parties, for instance. You had to move around. You couldn't hold the arm of your wife like a scared little boy. So he would be trapped in some part of the room in a tight circle of semi-drunks and he would look up suddenly to see Madge cornered by some white-collarad male with a drink in one hand, weaving close to her in a conversation that looked intimate, almost suggestive. It looked that way, but it could be perfectly innocent. Yet it was not the man but the twisted little smile that played over Madge's face along about the third drink, as if she was sharing an evil secret. Was it about him? Was she saying something about him he didn't even know himself? Some snide caricature? When he finally thought he had caught her eye with a warning look, she went right on talking, staring back at him in that sightless, glassy way, as though he were some kind, of poltergeist, gone suddenly invisible.

Then sometimes she would disappear into another room with one of these soap-opera males, or vanish to the lawn or patio. But when, with all apparent innocence, he would come upon them, they would be only talking with a look of physical separateness while seeming in some mental way to embrace in a lewd exploration of each other's bodies. It was hypnotic. It was frightening. And he had given up confronting her with it. She treated him disdainfully, as a child seeing ghosts. She made him feel the weakness of petty jealousy, the unworthiness of evil suspicion. And he could not put into words what he had seen and not seen.

And then one night at a vacation beach party on the Florida coast in winter, he had missed her again. About half the crowd was swimming, the other half sipping cocktails on the lawn, dancing on the patio to a portable radio. When he couldn't find Madge, he got into a bathing suit and wandered down the beach, searching. Around a bend he saw naked figures in the moonlight, heard sly voices and giggling. One of the figures came to the edge of the water and stood a moment looking out to sea before stretching voluptuously, then racing after the naked man who had plunged into the ocean. The stretching figure was Madge! He was sure of it the long sweep of limbs, the high, firm buttocks, the marvelous tilt and swell of breasts. He was positive. No creature he had ever known could be put together in quite that way. It was Madge in nothing but a white bathing cap. The man, anonymous, tall, crudely muscular. But there were many tall men at the party, and a few were brawny.

He ran down the beach after them. He stood on the shore where they had entered. He shouted Madge's name, the sound of his voice falling apart in the wind. He went in after them. He was not a good swimmer. He soon tired and became a little panicky in the rolling darkness and vastness of the tepid ocean. Treading water, he was not even sure he saw a distant splash. He went back to shore and searched for the bathing suit he would recognize. He found nothing. A long stretch of clouds drifted across the moon and then he couldn't see fifty feet. He waited a long time. Finally he went slowly back.

When he arrived, Madge, fully clothed, a drink in her hand, was seated on a lawn chair, talking earnestly to the hostess. She was perfectly groomed and absolutely composed. She wanted to know, "Where on earth have you been?" For the first time in his life, he was a little uncertain of his sanity. Yet, when he managed to touch her hair by pretending an affectionate pat, it was slightly damp.

Later when he asked her, she said of course she had been swimming. If he had looked he would have found her with half a dozen others in the pool. He never said another word about it.

But he fell asleep now with a vague image of her in that startling moment when the moonlight marble of her stretched and flung into the ocean. And in his dreams, he improvised the intertwining of alabaster legs, sinuous beneath a dark tide of lonely water.

He came awake with the soggy impression of bell sound, a distant alarm clock wrongly insistent in the darkness near the bed. There should be the bright slant of sunlight. But still, the bell was ringing. The sound came and went, came and went. No. It wasn't the alarm. The phone. He groped around and found it on the night table, lifted the receiver, squinting at the luminous dials of the electric clock. It was three a.m. Exactly.

"Yes?" he said. "For godssake, who is it!" There was no answer, so he imagined that he had sleepily put the ear piece to his mouth. He slid his hand over the receiver. No, the position was correct. "Hello. Hello! What the hell! This some kind of joke?" He listened. There was a light hum and static of an open line. At first there was nothing else. Then by straining, now wide awake, he heard the regular sound of heavy breathing. He could not have said why, but the slow cadence of breath, the weird silence, held an unnerving aura of threat, a sly kind of evil waiting. He could almost feel the malice of a cunning mind, patiently revolving.

"Listen, you idiot," he said. "Just call once more and I'll find you and put you away where you belong!" He hung up.

"Who was that?" said Madge through the gauze of half sleep.

"Go back to sleep, honey," he said. "Wrong number."

She gave a little sigh and was quiet. He sat up in bed and smoked a cigarette. For a long time he was thoughtful. He tried to be calm, coolly analytical, as though this were some complicated but quite workable business problem. First the Buick and then the gas and lights, now the phone. There was enough. You could add it quite logically. Some crank. Someone he had fired, perhaps. A minor grudge that would run itself out. Anyone with the smallest power had enemies. It was one of the calculated risks of success. No real problem.

He would have been all right. He might even have gone back to sleep. But underneath the precise wisdom of his conscious thinking crept an illogical intuition, a certainty of real danger. So that in the end, he couldn't sleep and he couldn't bring into focus a single face to strengthen his intuition. But the face was there, somewhere in his past. And he was going to have to find it before very long. For the first time in years, he was frightened. More so because he did not know of what. He lighted another cigarette from the butt of the one in his mouth. His hand trembled ever so slightly. He knew one of the great reasons why he was frightened might have nothing to do with this thing that was happening. But only from those who have much, can much be taken away. . . .

Trying, out of long habit of control, not to hurry, he put on his robe and slippers deliberately and just as deliberately went downstairs, lighting the way before him to the den. From his robe pocket he took a key and unlocked the bottom drawer of his desk. From the drawer he took a blue steel .45 automatic pistol. He inspected the loading clip. He worked the slide, forcing a round into the chamber, then setting the gun at safety. Next he removed a metal box from the same drawer, unlocked it, and took from it only a large key.

Now he went through the kitchen and opened the cellar door. He flipped a switch and went down, the .45 clutched in one hand, key in the other. The only sounds were those of his slippers, a whispered padding on the stairs. He turned right and paused before a heavy oak door. He unlocked it with the key in his hand. He pressed another light switch. He was in a small square work room. There was a large bench containing a vice and electric saw. Over it, in brackets on the wall, a neat array of tools. He paid no attention to these. He touched something underneath the bench, pressing, pausing, pressing, again and again. There was a distant hum. And now with a thin, whining sound, a steel ladder dropped slowly to the floor. A dim light came from the square opening above.

He looked up. He put the gun in his pocket. There

was really nothing to fear. There was only one other person in the world who knew what was in the cubicle above. And if he couldn't trust Madge. . . .

He stood on the bottom rung. Slowly the ladder rose with him into the opening. He was carried as though on an escalator. When his body cleared the panel, it closed as it had opened, the light winked out and the room below was as before. Dark. And empty.

Chapter Three

*T*he tall man called Brick and whose full name was Sherman Hambrick, laid the cleaning rod on the kitchen table and shoved back his chair. "That'll do it," he said, and standing, took the rifle to the window. He opened the breach and held it toward the light, squinting down the barrel. He grunted. "Shines like a buck lieutenant's bars. A guy can get blood poisoning if he's hit with a slug from a dirty barrel. Right, Cal?"

Cal set down his coffee cup and smiled a humorless smile. "That's what I hear, Brick. You ready to use that?"

Brick returned the rifle to the kitchen table and stood with one foot on a chair, chewing a kitchen match and watching Barney eat. "What do you think, Barney?"

he said. "We ready to zero in with this thing?" He caressed the stock of the gun and dropped one eyelid in the barest fraction of a wink that was missed by Cal.

Barney grinned. "Bet your sweet ever-lovin'," he said. "I'm ready. Have been for years."

"Tonight then," said Brick. "Tonight!" His voice was like a door closing. He picked up the rifle and, grasping it beneath the trigger guard, tossed it horizontally across the table at Cal, who caught the barrel in the apex of thumb and forefinger just as it would have smashed against his face.

"What the hell!" he said. "What the hell, Brick."

Brick, standing tall with his hands on his hips, chuckled. "Just wanted to see if you were on the ball," he said. "Setup like this you have to think fast." The smile blew out in his face. "You're elected, Cal. I'm gonna lend you my friend there — just for the night. You're the best shot anyway."

"The hell you say. Why me? And why tonight?" Cal laid the rifle back on the table and began to knead his fingers.

"Because you've got even more to gain than we have," said Brick, the match bobbing in his mouth. "And tonight's as good as any."

"What more have I got to gain?" said Cal, leaning intently across the table.

"You inherit the woman," Brick said, half a smile returning to his face.

"Oh, crap!" said Cal and leaned back again in his chair.

"You don't want to play then?" said Brick casually. "You want out?"

"No, god damn it! I didn't mean that at all. I was just surprised that you thought I should . . ."

"Good! Then you'll trigger for us? Tonight?"

Cal lighted a cigarette and pinched the lobe of his ear. He looked down at the rifle. "All right," he said. "If that's the way you want it. I'm your boy."

"Good! said Brick again. He went over and stood with his big hands clutched around the window sill, looking out.

"What's the plan?" said Barney.

Brick was silent.

"What about the loot?" said Barney.

Brick turned. "That's a point," he said. "Maybe we shouldn't rush it. Afterwards it might be too hot to grab anything. Never thought of that." But he had. He had thought of that and every small detail. There was a purpose in everything he said and did. Even the baiting of Cal was part of a plan. "We'll wait," he said. "We'll still take it slow. And we'll use Cal in the part he plays best. With the woman. You like that, Cal? You like it better?"

Cal smiled his easy smile. "I don't like it better. But I like it plenty. In a different way."

"All right," said Brick. "You make contact. You can find a way."

"Maybe she's changed."

"Huh!" Brick snorted. "About five out of a hundred people ever change much in a whole lifetime." He was thinking that he was one of the five. "Anyway, that's your problem."

Barney pushed his plate aside and put his feet up on the table. He wiped his mouth with the back of a meaty hand. "How did he take the needle?" he said to Brick. "What'd he sound like on the phone?"

"He did a slow burn."

"Not scared?" Mouth open, his eyes wide in his flat face, Barney had the expectant look of one who stalks game in a strange country.

"Can't tell about that one," said Brick. "He's cool. On the surface. You remember."

"Yeah. Cool. But when we step down hard on him, he'll crack like thin ice. The sonofabitch."

"He'll crack," said Brick. "They all do. You find out where they live and that's where the ice is thin." He rammed a big fist in his palm. "My God, how I want to see him get it!" He turned back to the window.

"He lives in his pocketbook," said Barney.

"Partly," said Cal. "And a big part in the woman."

"You'd know about that," Barney said with a sly grin.

"I'd know about that," said Cal. But he didn't smile.

"He's gonna pay," said Brick. "Jesus, but he's gonna pay for those stinkin' years. He's gonna set us up like playboys for the rest of our lives. Notice where he went after the call? Right down to the basement. Couldn't have beer, over half an hour. That's where he keeps it all right." He came back to the table and picked up the rifle, cleaning the telescopic lens with a handkerchief.

"That room where he went," said Barney. "No windows. I tried the other side of the house and couldn't see a thing."

"He must be worried," said Cal. "Carrying that gun."

"He's only begun to worry," said Brick. "And he'll never get to use the gun."

"What's on the program for him today?" said Barney. "I mean besides the creepers. I've got that all set."

"We'll coast with him till after we crack the basement," Brick said. "Then we'll shove it in and break it off. Who's got the keys to the Ford?"

"I have," Cal said.

Brick reached out his hand. Cal fumbled in his pocket, produced the keys and dropped them in Brick's palm. Brick passed the rifle to Barney. "Break it up and put it away," he said. He went to the door, turned. "Cal. You get dressed nice and pretty. When I get back, be ready with an angle. It should look like you just happened to bump into her."

He opened the door. The other two still didn't ask where he was going. He went out.

After the door closed, Barney Sykes, the squat, meaty one who had come all the way from California, waited until he was sure Brick was out of earshot. Then he said to the other, Cal Morgan, "Where you think he's goin', Cal?"

Cal shrugged. "You never know about him."

"That's for sure," said Barney. He gave Cal a shrewd look. "You don't like him much, do ya?"

"We're all in this together," said Cal carefully. "I like him all right. You can't beat him for this kind of stuff."

"You're afraid of him," said Barney.

"I have a healthy respect for him," Cal said. "There's a difference."

These were just words to Barney. He was afraid of Brick himself and he wanted to know he had company. "Nah," he said, "You're just plain scared of him. You take orders from him like he was top kick and you was buck private."

Cal grinned. "What're you trying to prove, Barney? Seems to me you turn into a little lamb when he's around. You take your share of crap without any argument."

"I don't take crap from no one," said Barney. "I let him run the show 'cause he knows what he's doin'. He's sharp. Course, I wouldn't wanna cross him. He's a tough bastard. Plenty tough. And mean.''

"Yeah," said Cal, stretching and getting up from his chair. "Got to shave and take a bath."

Barney leered. "Look pretty for the dame, huh?"

"That's it," Cal said.

"Once for me," said Barney. "Once for me."

But Cal was already walking toward the bathroom and pretended not to hear. And Barney was just as glad to see him go. Because aside from the business at hand, he had nothing much to say to Cal. Morgan was a college man and that alone made Barney uncomfortable. And Morgan was good with words, phony smooth. And since he wouldn't talk much about his women and Barney didn't understand his big time, big shot ideas, what was there left?

Barney wasn't sure if he liked Cal. Sometimes he wasn't sure at all.

He got up now and lumbered into the kitchen. From the refrigerator he took two beers, uncapped them and went back to his chair. He sat one on the table next to him and began to pull on the other, taking big gulps and wiping the foam on the back of his hand.

He heard Cal running water in the tub and he thought of how Cal would soon be with the woman. This was what he wanted almost as much as the money and his revenge — a woman. It had been more than twelve years since he had felt the touch of warm female flesh. pressed against him, the quick, rocketing surge of release. And then it had been nothing more than a B-girl pickup, a cheap tramp taken in a scabby hotel room in a haze of booze.

Although he could not have put the feeling into words, Barney envied Morgan his tidy handsome features, his grand manner of educated speech and subtlety of approach, the key to easy familiarity with the kind of women Barney wanted and could least understand. In the presence of women like Madge Driscoll, Barney was an awkward bungler and read on their faces the hardly concealed distaste they felt for him. He was too blatantly physical, too crudely obvious to cope with the circuitous fencing and virtuous posing of the Madge Driscolls.

He covered his feeling of inadequacy with a brash disdain. Men of refinement were "sissies" and women "snobs." Yet when, on the few occasions he was accepted by those he secretly considered superior and was treated with kindness, he was full of respect and admiration. A man became a smart cookie, plenty on the ball. A woman had class. She was a lady.

He was in the middle with Cal. He was unable to paste any label on Cal, even in the privacy of his thoughts. On the one hand Cal seemed to accept him as an equal, and an the other to hold some part of himself in reserve so that Barney was never quite sure if, he knew Cal at all. Cal had gone to college. Cal came from middle-class parents of some means and higher education. Thus he was already removed. And Cal had a special knowledge of all but the roughest types of women, placing him still another space apart. Barney was already jealous of him and would only have to cross a thin line to hate him.

Barney was a former truck driver for a moving van line out of Los Angeles. He made long, weary, cross-country hauls and was away from home more than he was present. But he was well paid in his job and it was his pleasure to announce that white-collar workers were jerks since he earned fifty dollars more a week than most of them and as-much or more than a lot of junior executives chained to desks in stuffy offices.

During the time just before he was drafted into the army, Barney had met and fallen for a girl whom he considered several notches above him. She was a book-keeper in the office of the van line. She had gone to UCLA and her family were humble but "nice" people. They had at least the appearance of refinement, lived in a modest but cleanly modern development in Venice. The father was a CPA.

The girl's name was Mary Tucker and he adored her. He worshipped her. He had never known anyone like her. She represented the major achievement of his life. She took him in like a dirty gray cat who had scavenged for years in back alleys and fed him warmth and kindness and acceptance. She made him feel a part of her and of her family. She promised to marry him.

In truth, Mr. and Mrs. Tucker were secretly not too pleased with the match. They had scrimped to send Mary through UCLA for more reasons than education. But Mary was one of those incurably plump girls with small unattractive features that threatened always to be swallowed by flesh. She was a sweet girl and intelligent, but one who seldom had a date unless it was blind as old Tom at the corner newsstand. So, Mr. and Mrs. Tucker had settled for Barney almost gratefully.

But when Barney was drafted, the Tuckers advised Mary to delay the marriage until his return. Their reasons were the usual ones — that the couple could not establish a home, have children, financial security or live any kind of normal life until the end of the war. But behind closed doors, the Tuckers discussed the possibility that while Barney was away, Mary could be shamed into losing about twenty-five pounds and then some more likely young men could be wined and dined for her benefit. In any case, they had sized up Barney as a man who would be always available. Mary bowed to the wisdom of her parents and Barney departed with a promise of marriage when he returned.

But Barney did not come back after the war. And though Mary had lost fourteen pounds, still the Tuckers had not found her a suitable husband. In fact, Mary remained stubbornly faithful. Until Barney wrote of the trouble that would still keep him away for endless years. That was when her parents were able to sow doubt and discontent. In two years, Mary married a successful lawyer fifteen years her senior, and, within the next four years, had three children.

That was when the small eye of faith inside Barney Sykes closed. That was when bitterness became a cancer of hate. And that was when Brick was able to turn the full force of that hate upon Driscoll.

Driscoll represented everything Barney despised — wealth, power, education. And he possessed what Barney might never have, the tall, coolly aristocratic lady with the sensual body — Madge Driscoll. Driscoll would pay for the fat years in the big clean house with the big-breasted snob of a lady in the warm bed.

Barney drained his beer and thought of the money. God almighty! With the kind of dough Driscoll must have socked away you could buy anything. Any god damn thing your eyes looked at in any god damn direction, you could buy.

Food? Hell, yes! You could buy a whole damn restaurant, a big steak house. And then you could clear the joint out and you could clap your hands and the flunkies would come running. And they would all stand around your table to wait on you. Just you. Barney Sykes. Maybe the help would be women. Waitresses. And there would be at least a couple of good lookers. And you wouldn't have to fool around with no pussyfoot games, neither. You'd just say, "You can knock it off now, blondie. Climb outta that uniform and be ready to step in ten minutes. And don't keep me waitin', ya hear?" Man! What a deal.

Cars? Hell, yes! Two, maybe three. About a block long. And fast. Nothin' faster but the dames on the seat next to you. God damn top down, sweet Florida wind in your face, redhead with long hair blowin' back, a big-money grin on her face for Barney Sykes.

Maybe later a house on the water, coupla maids, both cuties, and for the long haul, one of them droopy-eyed, long-legged, bigcanned bitches with the snob manners — like Driscoll's wench.

Damn right. That green stuff buys anything or anyone in any damn direction you can look.

His arm dangling over the side of the chair, Barney let the beer bottle slip from his grasp and fall to the floor where it rolled away, drooling beer like saliva across the rug. He took the other bottle from the table and began to slug it down.

Hope it goes right, Barney thought. Hope it cuts clean with no hitches. I don't know. Wanna see that black bastard, Driscoll, creamed good. Like to look down on him dead and spit on him. But I don't know. Like is one thing and doin' is another. Risky. You get caught and they chop you down and then what good is your pile of dough?

Maybe Brick don't mean to blast him for keeps — just scare him stupid, then work him over so he won't never forget.

You can't tell about Brick. You can't figure what he's thinkin'. He's got a twelve-year mean on. Mean. All mean inside. Maybe a little crazy, too. Something went wrong with him a few years back. Something got loose inside him. Crazy. Plenty cool. But crazy.

Barney heard the bathroom door open and when he looked up, Cal, all slicked down and sissy dressed for the woman, had come inter the room.

"What's keepin' Brick?" Cal said.

Chapter Four

*B*rick sat in the fifty-two Ford sedan which Cal had bought with part of Brick's money, socked away against the end of the sealed, grinding years. He had found Iroquois Park and had wound up to the top, pulling off the road in a stone-walled area where you could look down upon the city.

He had wanted to be alone. He was tired of talk. Too much talk drained away some of the power that he had stored in lonely hate for action. After it was over, he would separate from them anyway. He had come to have less and less use for and need of people. Even the ones he called his friends. He enjoyed the sullen, brooding company of his own thoughts. And anyway, while most people were fumbling with stupid questions, he had come up with sharp answers. The sharp edge of his mind cut away the fat of small talk with its idle speculation and slobbering emotion.

There had been a time, so long ago now, when he had not been as dry and brittle as a fallen twig under a parching sun, when a warm river of affection and boyish enthusiasm for the whole adventure of life had coursed through him. That was during the time of Louise "Lou" Hambrick, the married time with the apartment on Riverside Drive, the easy friendships, the glib sales job with the big insurance company on lower Madison. He was moving fast then. A man high on top of his competition, he was being talked about as the one likely candidate for supervisor of an important district.

But Lou, an angular, dark-haired Southern girl with deep, quiet eyes and soft speech, was the hub of his affection, the seat of his trust. And when the war had chapped them apart, with brutal suddenness destroying the whole dream, short-circuiting success, she had waited in her quiet way, filling the mails with her gentle, childish letters. And even when the strange, bitter thing had happened, she had hovered in the background, taking a job with a publishing firm to wait out the long years with apparent calm and a certain stoical faith.

But after a few years, the letters stopped and he was helpless to find out why. When he returned, she was gone, so long gone that even the broken threads of her life were beyond tracing.

That was the last time of his loneliness. For when he couldn't find her, even the need of her or of anyone left him. His emptiness was filled with a new and terrible strength of self-completion.

The plan had taken shape during the first time of real bitterness after her letters had stopped, had become irrevocable after the fruitless search for her in New York. In her absence, it was convenient and necessary to turn the full force of his hatred, the full blame for betrayal, upon the one tangible enemy — Gregory Driscoll.

Even so, he was a man of careful judgments and there was still left to him a certain objective balance. He was too clever to allow the emotion of revenge the quick, passing smile of a killing. Especially since after that temporary satisfaction might come his own destruction. He was wise enough to know that there is small revenge in instantaneous death, that like the prisoner awaiting execution, the real punishment is in the conscious fear

of his end. He much preferred the slower agony of in-
sinuating terror without the foolish necessity of that
dangerous climax.

But his plan would be almost ridiculous unless it
included the carrying away of a lasting reward, the
riches that would in time erase the memory of his suf-
fering. And he could not take a fortune from Driscoll
without fear of discovery. The man was knowing, intui-
tive. He was a thinker. He had imagination. Sooner than
later, he would figure it all out. He would come up with
faces. And the faces would grow names. He would see
that the secret must have passed from the woman and
no other. And he would squeeze the truth from her.
Then, armed with names and facts, he would be relent-
less. You could not run far enough from a man like
Driscoll. You could never be easy while you waited for
the clanging of a steel door. And Brick, so long as he
lived, would never again be confined by any man. So
that beyond revenge, in the cool analysis of the facts, it
was only self-protective that Driscoll should cease to
exist.

And now he was thinking about the others, Cal
Morgan and Barney Sykes. He was thinking about the
risk of any plan which included dependency on anyone
but himself. His strength, his immovable determina-
tion, were known to him. They were proven factors. But
how could you be sure there was not some hidden weakness in another?

About Barney Sykes he could be quite certain.
There was something primitive about Barney. He was
not complex. He was not even imaginative. He was
predictable. The simple lines of his character, the basic
emotions were on the surface to be read like headlines
of a tabloid. He had the animal instincts of blind loyalty
and savagery. You had only to train him to hate and

obedience, then at a given moment, turn him loose.

Cal Morgan was another matter. He was smooth and polished. He was subtle. He could look into the face of a man or woman and discover behind the eye that secret shadow of thought with which to determine his next course of speech or action. He understood the fragile interplay of human relations. His reactions were quick and discerning. Thus, as with shrewd politicians, you could never be sure until the last what swift current might move him off in another direction.

For that very reason, Brick had provided the test. Without warning, he had elected Cal executioner. And he had set the time for now. And since ordinarily Brick held a pat hand, had never been caught in a bluff, it was a true test. All the chips were down. Cal had not failed. He had reacted with a proper astonishment. But then he had swung slowly to acceptance and finally, positive agreement. There would have been no out for him. He would have to take that gun in his hand and fire that shot.

If for one moment I doubted the bastard . . . thought Brick. But I don't. He swallowed the hook and didn't squirm. He's slick. But he's safe. And my God, we need him. He's the key.

Brick started the motor, backed and wound down the hill. As the cool green trees of the park fled past, he was thinking that the hardest part had come. The waiting. They had probed Driscoll just enough. They had teased the first reaction out of him. They had given him the feel of danger. And like a man who smells smoke in the house, sees the first tongue of flame lick the darkness below, he had gone to inspect the safety of his treasure. This was as planned. This was expected of him. They had watched and he had revealed this much — that the basement held the answer, that the money was still in the house. And how it must have grown over the years!

Enough. Now they must wait. Too much scare and the loot would be removed. The next, the only quiet chapter, belonged to Cal. And then, though it was risky, they could not be denied the pleasure of the final terror.

Even now, Brick was thinking of a way to prolong it.

Chapter Five

Cal Morgan waited in the Ford a full block down the tree-shaded street from the Driscoll place. He sat easily behind the wheel smoking a cigarette. It was a pleasant atmosphere in which to spy. The dense overhang of tall trees formed a leafy roof against the midday sun and, for once, let the faint breeze stir cool air. There was silence along this side street with its remote and tidy dwellings rambling and rising splendidly from the chlorophyl crests of immaculate lawns. The only sounds were whisper-quiet bird mutterings, wind breathings and now and then the distant, muffled echo of a child's voice at dignified play. It was all so unworldly, a kind of fairyland escape from anything so dreary as toil, so unclean as poverty.

It was even hard to believe that mere money had

bought this sanctuary. And yet, money had and would buy most of the sanctuaries of the world — except those of the mind. Money bought tree-shaded coolness in the center of sickening heat. Money bought space and privacy from the shoulder-jam of the sweating crowd. Money bought placid silence in the midst of the strident, bickering city. It bought the shine of new things and paid people to keep them clean against the sordid dirt and decay of the tired masses. It made for convenience and ease from a thousand annoyances. You took a taxi instead of a bus. Or were driven in your own splendid car. You phoned the grocer instead of pushing a cart in the surge of penny-savers at the supermarket. You bought a case of the best instead of a fifth of a cheap blend. When things became old, broken or soiled, you didn't make do. You ordered them removed from your sight and replaced with the new, the improved.

And money had abstract uses. It made sin more secret and convenient. And more frequent. It wasn't even called sin. It was (with a wink) an eccentricity, a whim, a diversion. Simply the rich at play.

Yes, money had many uses. And waiting in the second-hand Ford, Cal liked them all. Looking around him, he was more firmly convinced that he was very fond of money.

Madge would sweep out of the drive any moment now and turn the other way. And he would follow. A few careful inquiries had disclosed that on Thursday afternoons she consorted with the common people to the extent of taking in a movie on Fourth Street. Gregory Driscoll had no time for the silly dream escape of pictures and so she went alone every Thursday. But Cal was quite sure that she was merely bored and could be redirected if she should just happen to bump into him. So he waited in his natty slate-blue tropical, complete with black and white sport shoes, his scrubbed hand-some features bland and innocent of guile. Meanwhile, his thoughts turned again to Brick and some of the joy crept out of him.

The verbal duel with Brick had been close. He had almost come undone there for a moment when Brick tossed the gun and ordered him to do the killing. This was a thing he had wanted to avoid. He had always said he was "a lover, not a fighter." And essentially this was true.

In his way, he had as much hate for Driscoll as they did. But he had really supposed that most of the talk of killing him was a kind of release and in the end they would be quite satisfied with frightening him half to death and taking his money. It was the money that interested Cal first and last. The scare campaign was intriguing but secondary. It was even a little childish, since to Cal the best revenge was one he could spend and the other a kind of reprisal that would hardly reward him for the loss of twelve good years of life.

Madge was the real bonus. He was very anxious that Driscoll should be tortured with her. This he under-stood. But murder was frightening.

Why he didn't speak out blatantly against shooting Driscoll, Cal didn't quite know. But without ever voicing a threat, there was something so intensely violent, so quietly menacing about Brick, that Cal was afraid of him. It was no simple fear, either. It was a sick dread of crossing him. Brick had once been a man. But now, he was a force. He carried with him an aura of command and purpose that could lead a thousand, ten thousand men to some mob cruelty. And the force of him could explode inward as well as outward. It was ready to strike, had to strike at something. Cal Morgan did not want to explore that force.

He was content now to delay, to improvise with the situation. There was Madge and, above all, the money. After the money, he would want out and he would find a way.

There had always been a way out for him. Until, he thought wryly, they closed a door he couldn't open twelve years ago.

His had been a smooth but careless road. His family had always provided just enough money for him to hang on the rim of luxury and want more and more.

After college, the textile firm of his brother-in-law gave him a job in advertising and sales promotion. The job demanded not too much, the pay was excellent and there was travel to department stores around the country, setting up new gimmicks for their line. In effect, he was on his own and this he liked.

But he was always restless, dissatisfied. For a man of his taste and intelligence there should be much larger horizons. He dreamed of setting up his own advertising agency. To save that kind of money from his salary was ridiculous. He began to gamble, shuffling his itinerary so that he was habitually at the scene of a going race track.

His losses became so constant that they ate up all of his expense allowance and his salary. One way or another, he was in debt in most of the major cities of the country. He owed great sums to his sister and brother-in-law, lesser amounts to his father and a dozen or so women around the country, each convinced he would be back , any moment with the marriage license.

Drinking heavily, about to lose his job, he determined to peel off the past. He was going to crawl slowly back to success and integrity. He was doing to repay with interest all who had loved and aided him.

It was an immense task but he made a good start,

was promoted, and began to pay his debts. And liked himself for the first time in his life.

Then overnight the whole thing was shot to hell. He was drafted. And, from the beginning, it went badly. He went in with a rebellious spirit. He was angry because he had begun to feel solid man in himself. He was moving up and playing the game by the rules when — chop! — they took it all away from him.

He despised the army. The drab, brutal life with its narrow regimentation filled him with despair. The surly authority of infant minds rankled and abused his intelligence until he showed such disdain for regulations, he was always in some minor trouble just this side of the guard house.

Then there was the nightmare invasion of Jap — held Pacific Islands, his return to the States and his affair with Madge Driscoll.

And, during the time of Madge Driscoll, the real trouble began.

He turned his attention back to the distant driveway. And, as he watched, he ran an old picture through his mind, intimate scenes of Madge as she had been long ago. It was not a picture for children. He was creating a mood, making her familiar and pliable in his mind so that he would be ready for the part he was about to play.

And then the black Thunderbird shot out of the driveway and made a tight turn, disappearing like some scurrying beetle. Warming his motor, he waited until it swung right at the highway intersection, then followed.

He kept well behind her for a couple of miles. Then as they neared town and the traffic grew thicker, he caught her just as a light flashed red. He pulled abreast.

With apparent idle curiosity, he turned his head slowly in her direction. Her neatly brushed hair seemed a shade darker than the Thunderbird. In profile, her face had the clear-skinned, clean-lined definition of all beautiful women. The thrust of her lower lip gave her a slightly sullen look. Like the spoiled wealthy, her face looked slightly put out about the whole thing. As though the mechanical process of going from here to there without simply materializing were a bore and a nuisance. She did not seem older to Cal. The word was mature. She had filled out some. But she was ageless.

He played the game. He was now noticing a lovely stranger in a trim Thunderbird convertible. Being a man, he was curiously killing time, looking at a woman. But now as he looked at the woman, she seemed familiar. His eyes widened as his thought groped for a name. The name was on the tip of his tongue. Meanwhile, his gaze was intent and she was feeling it. There! She was turning slowly. Her eyes were full of cold contempt for a masher. But the frankly puzzled expression on his face was forcing her to study him more closely. She was frowning. Her mouth was opening. It was the exact moment.

"Madge!" he shouted. But the light had changed and his voice was lost in the roar of her departure. Yet she had slowed and was looking back, leaning out the window. He drew next to her. Both cars stopped.

"Madge!" Madge Driscoll. It is you, isn't it?"

She was nodding.. "Yes. I'm Madge Driscoll. But I can't quite . . ."

"Cal Morgan. Remember?"

"Cal who?"

"Morgan. Morgan! Look ma, no uniform and twelve years older. Now do you remember? The soldier and the Captain's wife?" It was a little crudely put, but it would awaken her. Her face flickered, then warmed suddenly.

"Cal. Cal! It can't be. What a shock! I thought you were still in — in the army."

"Not any more."

"What on earth are you doing here?"

"Same as before. Advertising promotion. Textiles. I check our line in department stores around the country. Do a lot of traveling. Must we talk here?"

She seemed momentarily. flustered, turning away, then back again. "I — we live just a mile or so from here."

"Is that so? How nice, he said with intended vagueness. He waited. It was better to let her take the lead.

She chewed on her lip. "I was just going to a dull movie. I can skip it. Would you like to come up for a drink?"

"Sure. I was just cruising around, looking over the town."

"We go back the other way," she said. "Just swing around and follow."

"Right!" he called.

She waved and was gone in a forbidden U-turn. He followed, amused to think that she would never know how well he understood the way.

Chapter Six

*H*e followed her up the drive and parked his car next to hers in the three-car garage. He made special note that she hesitated a moment and then closed the garage door before taking him into the house. It's starting, he told himself. It's starting again.

"No servants today," she said. "They're off and we fend for ourselves on Thursday." They were in the den and she was behind the bar, uncorking a fresh bottle of bonded bourbon.. She jiggled ice and poured highballs, brought a tall glass to his chair. She was wearing a white sweater with a black and gold crest, a charcoal-gray skirt that flowed over hips, the tight sweep of thighs and legs, like a sheath. The long thrust and tilt of her breasts nodding beneath the sweater as she walked, made him feel almost faint.

He took a swift gulp of the liquor. It was quite a jolt. He should have known from the color that it was triple strength.

"Well," she said. "This is amazing. What a surprise!" She dropped into a chair and pulled down her skirt with a primness that belied that sensual body.

"Yes," he said. "The kind of surprise I like. How's it been with you?"

"Honestly?"

"Honestly."

"Dull."

He looked around. "This seems anything but dull."

"Just background music," she said. "Nothing much in the foreground."

"No startling changes?"

"None that show."

"I see. You don't *seem* to have changed."

"I haven't really. I've put on a little weight. Isn't it awful?"

"I like it." He tried to sound merely polite.

"You haven't gained," she said. "But you do look somehow — different. I can't say now. Let's see. You certainly are pale. What happened to the outdoor look? I mean — Oh God, Cal. I'm sorry. What a thing to say. After all, you . . .''

"It's all right," he said.

She twirled the ice in her glass and studied him in silence. The first shadow of intimacy crossed her face. "I don't understand," she said. "I don't understand at all. I thought you were — Is it all right if we talk about it?''

"I don't mind."

"Greg said that you — that you . . .''

"Got life?"

"Yes."

"I did."

"But they reduced it?"

"After the war. To twelve years."

"Oh, thank God! I — I feel like crying."

"Don't. It's all over."

"He never told me," she said.

"He didn't stay in after the war, did he, the good Captain?''

"Hardly a minute after," she said.

"Then he wouldn't know. I mean unless he inquired after my well-being.''

"Hardly. Oh, Cal. Dear Cal. I'm so glad for you. Such a cruel thing. And the others — they got out, too?''

"Yes."

"How are they?''

"All right, I guess. Haven't seen them since. Except for Leavenworth, and a mutual disgust with the army, we never had much in common.''

"I suppose," she said. "I never knew them. Twelve years. How did you ever stand it?''

"It's a kind of death. You shuffle from here to there with your body. But you're really dead.''

"I still want to cry," she said. "I hated him, you know. Oh, how I hated him."

"And now?"

"You can't go on hating."

"Can't you?"

"I got over it. I mean, I never forgot. I never could feel quite the same about him again."

"But you stayed with him."

"Yes, because after all, he didn't know about us. And in my own way, I was guilty, too. And I once loved him. It was the only thing that ever came between us — you — and what he did to you. I'll never understand. Because he always seemed so kind to me. But he was so dedicated and he thought he was doing his duty."

"Huh!" Cal snorted. "Listen, how could you have loved us both?"

"There are different ways of loving," she said. "One is a flame — and the other is an ember. One burns you up and the other just keeps you warm."

"Which one?" said Cal, smiling.

Her eyes dropped, came back to his. "The flame."

"Still burning?" he asked.

She was silent.

"How long have you been out now?" she said then. "Let's see, it couldn't be very long."

"Just a few weeks."

"And you got your old job back? I would have thought that they — There I go. I'm sorry."

"It wasn't so difficult. Because my sister's husband is quite a wheel there." Cal finished his drink and felt the first sensual flush of alcoholic well-being.

"Well, I'm glad. Another drink?"

"Why not?" He smiled. "Only about half the bottle this time."

She came over for his glass. He held it close to his

body so that she would have to lean down a bit to get it. Their eyes met and held. Neither smiled. Her lips parted slightly, as though in wonder, her eyes glazed over with fascination. Unmoving, she seemed to grow toward him. Without taking her gaze from him, she groped for the glass and when she had it, something went out of her eyes, her face closed and she turned away abruptly.

He followed her, leaning against the bar as she fumbled the drinks with nervous distraction. She laid the filled glasses on the mahogany surface and pushed them toward him. He picked his up, but when she came around to get hers, put it down quickly and blocked her path. She lifted her head and again she looked at him, biting the bright puff of her lower lip, her eyes sliding away from him.

He reached an arm around her waist and slowly pulled her against him.

"Don't," she murmured. "It's all different now. I have a child ten years old."

"That changes nothing," he said. "Nothing," he whispered against her ear, the hungry feather-pillow swell of her breasts against him, the press of her thighs, the bourbon glow, dropping him out of control.

She had been pulling away, but now suddenly she collapsed against him. As if on cue, he brushed his lips across her cheek until his mouth found hers and clamped over it. One hand climbed the soft hill of her breast, the other wound soothingly down hex back.

It was he that undid the kiss at last. But even then, she remained, eyes closed, head uptilted, lips parted. "You're right," she said hoarsely. "Nothing has changed. Nothing at all. I'm lost now. All lost." She squeezed her eyes tighter. "Don't let me be found. Don't let me think."

She took his hand and led him in sleep-walking

silence up the stairs. She entered a bedroom and closed
the door as gently as if someone were asleep in the room.

"It's been so long," he said.

"Don't say a word," she murmured, and there was
only the wooly whisper of her sweater as she pulled it
slowly over her head. And when her hands reached
around and fingers sought the clasp of brassiere, he
undid it with one swift motion. And when it fell to the
floor, he remained behind her. His hands drifted up
from her hips and closed over her swelling breasts as her
head swung around for a hungry kiss. She sank back
upon the bed, and brought him with her.

"*H*ow will it end this time?" she said long later, sleepy-
voiced, her head in the bare hollow of his shoulder.

"It won't be the same at all," he said. How true, he
thought.

"You mean you won't leave me?"

"I don't know. That's up to you. You have your own
life. I never was any real part of it." His mind was
functioning again, back on the plan, but now with immense clarity. The sensual, alcoholic fuzz had lifted. But
even so, he wished to take Driscoll's place in her bed
and at once assume all the other advantages. And this
without the necessity of any scheme or dangerous involvement. It should just happen because she agreed.

"You must always be a part of my life now," she
said. "I'll find a way. Because I love you, darling."

"I've always loved you," he said. "Like no one." He
said this with great sincerity because he was beginning
to think it was true. "But you have Driscoll."

"You and Greg are words apart."

"In what way?" He tried to sound disinterested. He
wanted to leave her with the feeling that she told all and

he asked nothing.

"He's a kind of self-wound, self-controlled machine." She sat up slightly and propped a pillow behind her head. "I admire and respect him. But he doesn't stir any feminine response."

"Desire?"

"Yes. Not much at all. He doesn't need me. How can he? He's a walking fortress against need."

"Fort Knox?"

She laughed. "Fort Knox."

"He must have a one-track mind to accumulate so much."

"Not entirely. It's the by-product of a big game he plays. The money is. He'll still be piling money when he has enough to buy the world. In some odd way he must be insecure. Otherwise. Otherwise, why . . ."

"Why what?"

"Nothing."

"Secrets."

"Not really. I told you long ago. I mean, otherwise why would he have to keep a fortune in that strange room when it could be earning interest at the bank?"

"Oh, yes. I remember. You mean the room in the basement?"

"Yes. My God! Did I tell you that? I don't remember telling you it was in the basement."

"Sure you did. You told me everything, angel." She hadn't told him about the basement at all, just the room. It was a bad slip.

"I guess I did at that," she said. "And I've never told another soul in the world. That's how carried away I was."

"Well, it's just a fascinating quirk," he said. "But not important."

"Oh, yes it is. To him."

"You don't care about the money?"

"Of course. But enough is enough. He's been adding to it all these years. A big green mountain."

"I wouldn't think it would be very wise to keep all that cash at home," he said.

"Only in theory," she said. "It's quite safe. You have to press a hidden button even to get into that room."

"So? Anyone can press a button."

"Yes, but it's like a combination. You press so many times, wait, then press again until you work it out. Then when you get inside, you have to know the combination of the safe."

He chuckled. "Well, anyway, if you run short of cigarette money, you'll know where to go."

"I've only been in that room twice in my life," she said. "With him. I don't even know the combination to the safe. He took me up there but he never opened it in my presence."

"He doesn't even trust you, then," Cal prodded.

"Oh, he probably does. I know he uses the numbers from his license plate to open the room. The safe is his big secret and I've never asked how to open it or how much is there. Why should I care? I have everything I need."

"Well," he said. "Driscoll is a strange one. Let it go at that." Slowly he fitted himself against her and she slid down until their mouths met in a long kiss. Then she yawned. "I feel so drowsy," she said. She snuggled against him. "And so cozy."

"Close your little eyes," he said softly, rubbing her back. "Just relax. That's my girl."

"Don't let me go to sleep," she said. "Whatever you do, don't let me go to sleep. It would be so easy."

"You sleep if you want to," he said. "I won't close

my eyes. I wouldn't dare."

"No," she mumbled against him. "That would be the end." And promptly, she fell asleep.

Chapter Seven

Cal eased gently out of bed. Quickly he pulled trousers and shirt over, his naked body, slipped bare feet into shoes. From his coat pocket, he produced two small metal instruments called pick and tension bar. These were clutched in his hand when he closed the door softly behind him. He raced soundlessly down the carpeted stairs, found the kitchen and the cellar door. It was partly open. He looked below. There was daylight enough coming from a pair of small windows. He went down.

He located the work room door easily. It was not a door two or even three men could shoulder down. He inspected the lock. It was formidable. But it was a type that could be picked.

He inserted the pick in the lock, worked it for awhile, finally sliding the tension bar in beside it and twisting the little handle until there was a small click. He turned the knob. The door opened. He groped for a switch, found it, but closed the door before lighting the room.

He was in a space no larger than a small bedroom. There was a workbench with an assortment of tools in brackets on the wall over it. Against the opposite wall were two cartons and a crate. Otherwise the room was empty.

He searched around for the button, wondering where it would be. He decided to the obvious first, ran his hand along the underside of the bench. He kept repeating the numbers of Driscoll's Buick license plate.

The numbers had been in his mind when, while Brick worked on the brakes, he had crawled under and removed the oil drain plug. He had known the car, but to be sure, he had checked the plate. The numbers were correct — three-nine-five-four.

His hand snagged on a small button underneath the right side of the bench. He hesitated. He wondered what special significance the numbers three-nine-five-four would have to Driscoll. Why would he have arranged to have them on his plate? Or was it the other way around? The numbers had been on the date and were used as the key to opening a hidden door. Cal didn't think so. The numbers probably had a special meaning in Driscoll's orderly mind.

About to press the button, he removed his hand as suddenly as if the button were on fire. It occurred to him that a man as ingenious, as Driscoll would have thought of everything. He crawled under the bench and searched the bottom surface, finding nothing. When he did find what he was looking for, a small knife switch, it was on the back side of one of the left, legs. He pulled the switch to center position and knew that he had broken the circuit to some kind of burglar alarm. When the button was pressed with the alarm in circuit, it might even flash a warning to some protective agency. That was a close one and from now on he would have to think a little faster than he moved.

He climbed from under the bench, brushed himself off and again reached for the button. He pressed out the sequence — three-nine-five-four — pausing between each number. And as he did this, he thought how impossible it would be for anyone to take Driscoll without the unwitting help of Madge. If you found the button in the first place, you could press it all day with sweepstake odds against success.

Having finished the run of numbers, he waited uneasily without the vaguest idea in which direction to look for a sliding door. He heard the thin, distant whine of a motor. But when it had stopped, then began again, he still saw nothing. Then he had the unnerving sensation of something dropping down upon him.

He looked up. His mouth fell open. He was astonished and even frightened to see a steel ladder descending from a mansized aperture which had opened in the ceiling. He stood absolutely rigid until the ladder had touched the concrete floor. Then he approached it and, looking up, saw a dim light. He hesitated, then placed his foot on the bottom rung of the ladder. Immediately there was the repeated whine of a motor and the ladder began to ascend. He placed his other foot on the rung just in time and was carried aloft.

His heart knocking against his chest, he still was able to observe that the ceiling was certainly much lower than the one of the basement proper and this would account for the space above.

He was still numb with shock when the ladder came flush with the floor above and the panel began to close slowly, shutting off the room below and plunging it into darkness. He hopped off obliquely and reached down to delay the sliding steel door. Too late.

He found now that he was sealed in a room about ten feet square which contained nothing but a great round-doored safe in its exact center, and an overhead light. And, though he searched minutely for a full ten minutes for some button, switch or lever, he could find no way out.

Driscoll had thought of everything.

Chapter Eight

*B*rick lay on his bed fn the room he had chosen for himself and tried to sleep. Whenever there was inaction, he tried to fortify himself with rest. Cal was with the Driscoll bitch, conning her for a clue to get at the dough, Barney was reading the paper in the living room and guzzling himself fat with beer. So there was nothing to do but wait. And while waiting, Brick was grabbing a few winks. No, he wasn't. He was only trying.

It was much too hot for sleep. The air was dense and breathless. The humidity threatened to smother him.

He tossed from one position to another, and finally, cursing, lay on his back and propped himself up with a pillow.

For a time his thoughts probed forward, sifting ways to squeeze Driscoll tighter, speculating on the amount of money and what he would do with his share, wondering if Cal would wrap that part up now so they could get on with the finish, the part he was going to enjoy best of all.

He tired of puzzling unanswerables. And, as they inevitably did, his thoughts drifted backward to the known, the motivating power of his hate.

He remembered when the godawful mess and stink of the war had changed for him, that all-too-brief period when it looked like he might sneak home safe to Lou and then maybe stay in the States until the dumb yellow bastards put away their toys and signed the papers. That's the way it looked.

And if not for Driscoll, it might have gone just that way.

*I*t began with luck. Really marvelous luck. Sergeant Sherman "Brick" Hambrick, U. S. Army Infantry, had come out of the battle for Saipan unscathed. That was the greatest of all luck since this was the third of such island-taking campaigns through which Brick had fought without death or injury. And this in spite of the fact that a good two-thirds of his rifle company had been killed or wounded on the blood-soaked Pacific islands.

But, though Brick was lucky because he had not been killed or wounded, he was unaware of his luck. He had expected to live and live whole. No other thought had ever occurred to him. Men died around him in disgusting fragments. Men were wounded and cried out in pitiful agony. Yet, he was like one of a mob who watched a gruesome accident. His view of life became degraded and cynical. But he was never a part of it.

No, the real luck for Brick was on the day of the lottery. It came shortly after the battle of Saipan while patrols were still mopping up small pockets of resistance — the cave-dwelling remnants of a Japanese army.

It was decided, as a small appeasement for dangerously restive troops more than two years in the Pacific without furlough, to send a detachment of three men from each company stateside. Since everything was "for the convenience of the government," these men had to have a purpose beyond a mere furlough. They were to be scattered among various stateside units of infantry virgin to combat. Their duty would be to assist in the training of these green troops in practical warfare. In due time, and all incidentally, they were to be awarded a thirty-day leave.

It was further decided, to avoid something like rebellion, that the group would be selected by lottery, three from a company. All enlisted men were eligible except those whose service was considered indispensible and those soldiers who were always in and out of the guard house or too incompetent to be useful.

Brick's name went into the hat. And when the three folded pieces of paper were lifted and spread open by the captain, his name was there. Also there were the names of Corporal Barney Sykes and Private First Class Cal Morgan.

With soaring spirits and undisguised relief, the threesome embarked on a troop ship for the long voyage home. However happy, it was a dull time of more waiting. And during the passage, Brick involved himself in the dozen or so crap games held in secret corners of the ship. Again he was lucky. When the ship docked in San Francisco, he had sweated thirty-six hundred dollars from the games, most of which he deposited in a bank on his first pass.

After a brief period of quarantine, the three were assigned to a fresh company of infantry at Fort Ord, below San Francisco, a company under the command of Captain Gregory Driscoll.

For a time, there was the pure joy of just being on US soil with an occasional twenty-four-hour pass. They waited quite patiently, content with fervent letters, each planning a fabulous reunion with wife, girl or family.

But as the days slid past and they could get only the vaguest answers from Driscoll about their expected furlough, the trio returned to their former sullenness and whining arrogance. Morgan was so obviously put out and uncooperative that he was assigned to the kitchen and there began the episode with Driscoll's wife.

Then suddenly it happened. They were struck dumb when one morning, along with other veterans, their names appeared on the bulletin board for reassignment. They were to be given not thirty-day furloughs but twenty-four-hour passes, then shipped immediately with an outfit being hustled overseas to a new engagement in still another unspecified combat operation.

Their angry and almost insubordinate complaints to Captain Driscoll were useless. He realized, yes he understood and was sympathetic with their problem, but however unjust it might seem, there was a war on, individuals had no rights and orders were orders. All veteran troops were needed in the line for some top-secret offensive. And that was that.

Brick had written his wife, Lou, not to come West, that he was expecting a thirty-day furlough at any moment. And now there was no time for her to come to him and he couldn't go to her.

And further, Brick, like the others, had been convinced that so far as he was concerned, the war was over.

And now the bravado, the conviction of safety held by the long untrammeled in combat, left him. He had that sneaking doubt that he would not live through another chapter, another invasion of still another fortress island of the Japs. For the first time, he saw himself gutted and glassy-eyed among the bloating dead, the lonely corpses huddled grotesquely on the sun-parched beach of a still nameless island. He could not and would not face it.

Barney and Cal were no less fearful and embittered. They agreed to meet with Brick in San Francisco to discuss a solution.

The final pass began on a Tuesday morning and was to extend to Wednesday at Reveille. Tuesday afternoon over Martinis atop the Mark Hopkins, the conversation which launched the trouble began. It was as Cal and Barney concluded a tirade of abuse hurled at the army and just before they had reached the brink of drunkenness that Brick, having listened in sullen silence, began to speak.

"All right," he said quietly. "Both of you shut up for a while and listen. You guys are full of crap. You talk and talk about what the army has done to you and what you're gonna do to it. When you get all through, you're gonna go right back and eat more crow until the crows eat you on some God-forsaken Jap island that isn't worth taking in the first place. Some god damn hole that a spit-and-polish general in Washington has found on a map with a ouija board. 'All right, boys,' he says, 'let's give this one a whirl. Good as any. They all look aike to me.' Sure, because he's never seen a Jap island, except on a map. So he says, 'Get the troops out on this one, Colonel. Make up an order in triplicate, and I'll sign it.' Jesus," Brick said, "they fight the war like a goddamn movie with them as producers sending the troops out on location. Only this is real, men. There's gonna be bodies lyin' around. And those bodies are gonna be yours. You think you're gonna come out of this one, Barney?"

"Hell, no," said Barney. "I've had it. If I come out

this time, it'll be in a box.

"You, Cal?"

"I don't know, Brick. You can push your luck just so far. I have the feeling mine's run out. Maybe one of us will come back with just an arm blown off. But I don't think it'll be me."

"You guys are suckers," said Brick. "Sheep. Dumb sheep to the slaughter. No one cares if you get your head blown off. Save your own head and after it's all over and they pull the flags down, most everyone will tell you — in private — you were a smart cookie. It's every man for himself. And the bright boys beat the rap. They stay home and screw the girls and make the dough like crazy and watch you in the newsreels. Wake up!"

"So?" said Barney. "What ya gonna do about it?"

"That's what I'm coming to," Brick said. He pushed his drink aside, glanced briefly around the room. He reached in his pocket and produced a choking roll of bills. "This is where it starts," he said. "Everything starts with money. I got three thousand here. A thousand a apiece and we can lose ourselves like three ants in an ant hill."

"You mean desert?" said Cal.

"I don't call it that, Morgan. But that's exactly what I mean. We just don't come back from these passes."

"You could get shot for that," said Barney.

"I doubt it," said Brick. "But they have to catch us first."

"What's the plan?" said Cal.

"Here's the way I have it figured," said Brick. "First thing we do is shed the uniforms for mufti. We go down to a store I know where they ask no questions and we get three pretty good ready-mades, shoes, shirts, ties, the works. Then we get a bottle and we lay low most of the time in a hotel room until Friday about nine-thirty in the p.m. At ten o'clock, we catch a fast train for New York. We're civilians traveling on business. We keep to ourselves. Friend of mine in New York owns a big machine shop on the Island. Phoned him last night. He needs men. He'll train us, give us jobs, high pay. He'll fix up phony papers for us under new names. You wouldn't get stopped once in a million times anyway."

"Sounds good," said Cal. "What about the train tickets?"

"Right in my pocket," Brick said. "All arranged. It only takes money, like I told you. But I couldn't get seats until Friday."

"By that time, we'll be about three days AWOL," said Cal.

"Don't let it bother you," said Brick. "If they catch us, we'll be a lot more than AWOL."

"Pretty sure of us, weren't you, Brick?" Barney said.

Brick put the roll of bills back in his pocket, stood up. "I go with you guys or I go alone," he said.

*A*t nine-thirty on Friday night, dressed in civilian clothes, each carrying an overnight bag containing nothing but their uniforms, toilet articles, and underwear, the trio walked briskly to the station. Here they drank coffee, black, and waited for the train to be called.

"What about MPs?" said Cal, his hand trembling slightly as he lighted a cigarette.

"There may be a few around," said Brick. "Expect it. Ignore the bastards. Mingle with the crowd. Look like one of the mob. You never heard of the war. You got problems of your own. You gotta pay extra for big steaks under the counter and black-market gas. You got servant problems. You got all this dough piled up and you can't even hire a decent servant. You're burned up about all this hardship and you got no time for anyone."

"Suppose they question us?" said Barney nervously.

"They won't, you dope. They won't! And if they do, just tell 'em how proud you are to have men like them, real stateside soldiers, fightin' the war of San Francisco for you. But you got no time for tea. You got to catch a train."

"I wish you'd stop kiddin' around," said Barney.

"I'm kidding because I want you guys to relax. Civilians are relaxed characters. The only shot they worry about is one that comes in a glass. There! You hear that? That's our train. Onward to freedom, men. Let's go!"

Brick led the way to the tail end of the crowd being fed slowly to the streamliner that would take them to freedom. They were lost in a sea of blank faces. The three looked very much like men of business, already a little bored in anticipation of a tiresome journey.

The exception might have been Barney. His bulky, irregular figure caused fabrics to tighten around the heavy shoulders, the great girth of his chest, while falling loosely in the gullies of his anatomy. And adding to this look of incongruity was a GI haircut — a fuzzy crewcut.

Nevertheless, even Barney would have passed all unnoticed had not a peculiar thing happened. As the crowd surged forward, a drunken soldier, tie askew, shirt flapping from his trousers, came from nowhere to join the surging crowd. He approached with a loose-jointed, stumbling gate, obviously drunk. His overseas cap was twisted oddly on his head, he wore a silly grin and sang loudly. Apparently he had no idea where the crowd was going. But it looked like fun. He mingled, shoved forward, fell, recovered and went on again.

"Jesus, God!" said Brick out of the corner of his

mouth. "Wouldn't you know? Just watch it now. Watch it!"

At this point, two MPs who had been passing on a casual inspection of the depot, saw, and moved in quickly. The tallest of the two was the sergeant in charge of one of the town patrol details. He moved with grace and lithe power. He had a face like cracked parchment.

It took only a moment to collar the drunk and remove him from the line. Now the sergeant, after a brief and apparently useless interrogation of the soldier, lifted his arm in signal. In a moment, two more MPs appeared. Walking ridiculously upright, they took the drunk away while the prisoner staggered between them. Meanwhile, the sergeant and his helper lingered.

As the line of passengers narrowed at the gate, it was impossible for the three deserters to pass unobserved by the MPs. Realizing this, they walked with a certain exaggerated casualness. Especially Barney, the worst of hams, who sauntered forward, his coat open, hands in his pockets. In fact, as Barneycamp abreast of the sergeant, the MP seemed to give him such a hard glare (actually it was the same look he gave everyone), Barney felt compelled to offer a small statement of praise.

"Nice work, sergeant," he said. "You men are the backbone of our country. We're proud of you."

The sergeant didn't smile. He didn't reply. His face never changed. But his eyes roved over Barney as carefully as a buck lieutenant inspecting the troops of his platoon before granting leave. And, as Barney was about to pass on with a condescending nod of approval, the MP said, "Just a minute, soldier!"

Startled, Barney turned with his mouth open, like a small boy caught stealing candy. He recovered quickly and tuned away with a mumbled, "Who you talkin' to, boy?'' He was about to move on with the other two when a hand reached out and steel-hard fingers closed around his arm.

"What the hell!" Barney said. "Let go my arm. You can't touch a civilian." The sergeant swung Barney around to face him. Meanwhile, the other two paused uncertainly to watch.

"A-tennn-shun!" the sergeant barked. Barney snapped his feet together in reflex response, but quickly slouched again and forced a smile. "I get it," he said. "You guys are pullin' a little gag. Sure. I used to be in the army. Medical discharge. Good fun, fellas, but now I gotta catch a train."

The sergeant maintained his gri while looking over Barney's shoulder at Cal and Brick. "Are you with this man?" he said, peering at one and then the other.

Cal looked at Brick but Brick stared directly at the sergeant of MPs. "No," he said. "Not exactly. We were walking with him and we struck up a conversation. Don't even know his name."

"Is that so?" said the sergeant sarcastically. "Don't even know his name. We'll see. Come back here and let's have a look at you two."

"No time, pal," said Brick. "Got to catch this train!" With that, Brick. and Cal began to walk rapidly away.

"Hold it!" the sergeant shouted. "Come back here!"

Brick turned. "You better not try to stop us, buddy. We're gonna make this train even if somebody gets hurt."

The sergeant loosened the flap of his gun holster, revealing the butt of his .45 service automatic. "Just don't try it," he said. "You'd never make it."

Brick and Cal returned slowly. "Before you fool with us, soldier," Brick said, "you better call the civilian police. We know our rights. You'll get yourself in a lot of trouble with your commanding officer."

"Maybe that's true," said the sergeant. "But until you prove to me that you're a civilian, I'm gonna treat you like a soldier. Because I'm beginning to think that's what you are. You men got belts to match this one, you're in trouble."

"Belts?" said Brick.

"What belts?" said Cal.

The sergeant pulled aside Barney's coat, revealing a tan brassbuckled belt with army emblem. "That belt looks like army to me," he said, as Barney looked down sheepishly. "Now, open them coats and let's see if you two can match it."

Brick and Cal only stood there, eying the sergeant coldly. The belts had been forgotten until they were dressing to leave for the train. It was then too late to buy replacements so it was decided this could be done in New York. Meanwhile, the belts would be concealed by their coats. But Barney had been careless.

"Well?" said the sergeant.

They stood there woodenly. A new tension had come into Brick's face. His eyes were dangerous as they measured the sergeant and his helper.

The long arm of the sergeant shot out. Knobby fingers close on cloth and jerked upward. A button of Brick's coat flipped off. The army belt was discovered.

"You shouldn't have done that, pal," said Brick. "That's where you made your big mistake." He took a step forward.

"You wanna play, too?" said the sergeant to Cal.

Cal opened his coat. "All right," he said. "So I've got one like it. They're a dime a dozen in any store. What does it prove?"

"To someone else," said the sergeant, "maybe it proves nothing. But I got a little friend running around in my head says it proves everything. First place it proves you three are together. Second place it proves you're probably on the way over the hill from the army. Deserters. One way to find out. I'm gonna have a nice long look at what kind of papers you got in your wallet and what's in them bags. Then if you don't shape up okay I'm gonna take you in and have your stories checked out right down the line."

"As of right now you're finished with us," said Brick "You're not takin' us anywhere."

"You don't think so?" the sergeant said.

"No."

"Why?" said the sergeant mildly.

Brick moved in close to the sergeant and, as if this were a signal, Barney and Cal stepped beside the other MP. "I'll tell you why," said Brick with a tight mouth. "Because we can't afford to let that happen. It would be the end for us. They might throw away the key. Or they might shoot us."

"What you're sayin' is that you're deserters," the sergeant said. "And I'll have to put you under arrest."

"Don't try it," said Brick. "You stateside MPs think you're hard — tall guys with big .45's. You don't know what hard is. While you've been playin' police stateside, we've been playin' war for keeps. We're trained to mangle guys like you with our bare hands. See what I mean?"

There was something so quietly malevolent about Brick that some of the sergeant's official confidence drained from his eyes. Yet all he said was "So?"

"So here's a tip, pal," said Brick. "We can take you. And we'll do it. Don't bother to look down at your gun. You'll never get a chance to use it. You won't get it out of the holster. Use your head. There's three of us here. All fighters. We can take you guys apart at the roots in ways you never heard of this side of the ocean. We'd have to kill you. We got nothing to lose. Is it worth it? Don't be a dope. You got it soft. See it out the easy way. We got our reasons. We got screwed — overseas a couple of years gettin' our tails shot off and then they won't give us even a ten-day leave and promised us thirty. Sending us right back out again. But you think of your hide first, pal. Think of your eyes pushed back in your head like peeled grapes. Let us go and nobody knows the difference."

"I think you *would* try to kill us," the sergeant said. "But you better go ahead and try. I can't let you get away."

"Not even if we walk into the men's room, change back to uniforms and go on to Ford Ord? You'd have our word on it."

"No," the sergeant said. "Not even then."

"Jesus!" said Brick "You got no heart at all. You don't leave us any choice but to maul you for keeps. All right, Barney, Cal. We're gonna have to cream these poor bastards."

The sergeant wet his lips. "Wait a minute," he said. "You ain't got all the cards. You gotta use your head, too. There's half a dozen MPs around. There's two right over there. See? They're coming now. And lots more on call. Show him the whistle, Joe."

Joe, the other MP, stuck a whistle in his mouth "Before you can move, he blows that whistle and they'll all be down on you. City cops around, too. You don't have a chance, fella. You play it our way and I'll give you every break I can. But I have to take you in."

At that moment, the two MPs who had taken the drunk. away, approached the group. "Stand back and draw your guns," the sergeant shouted. After a moment's hesitation, the newcomers pulled guns from holsters and waited. It was all over.

Soggy and restless on his bed in the southside apartment, Brick was thinking now of how they had been searched at the police station, their army identities discovered from papers in their wallets. Then the long, jolting night ride back to Ford Ord, flanked by a detail of MPs. And all the way they had pleaded with the sergeant to give them a break, telling their stories in detail to enlist his sympathy.

The sergeant, it turned out, had himself been wounded on Guadalcanal and was more than ready to admit. "You guys had it shoved in and broken off." But while the sergeant had cooled, he was by then committed to bring them in. Anyway, it was his firm belief that if their company commander wasn't strictly a by-the-book soldier, he would be disposed to reduce the charge to AWOL. He might even send them on to their troop ship which was still loading at a San Francisco dock. Didn't a CO have sovereign power over his own men?

Yes, thought Brick now, the bastard had sovereign power. And what he did with that power was, twelve years later, going to cost him his money and his life.

*H*ey, Brick!" Barney had poked his head in the door.

"Whatta you want?" said Brick, without turning to look at him.

"Cal shoulda been back by now. It's late. That Driscoll bastard might leave early for home. And Cal's over there. Least he said he was gonna steer the dame there so he could get at the dough in the basement."

"So?"

"So, maybe he got caught. Guy like Cal gets caught and they put fire under him, he's gonna talk. He talks, he tells where we are. Next thing you know they're breakin' down the goddamn door."

"You been drinkin' too much beer," said Brick, turning on his side. "If it was you over there; I'd worry. Cal can handle it. Be back any minute."

"Maybe," said Barney dubiously.

"And don't worry about Driscoll. He might even be a little late."

"Oh," said Barney. "You mean the present I dug up for him on the coast?"

"Yeah."

"That's right," said Barney, chuckling. "I forgot. He's gonna have company on the way home. Who knows, he might not get home at all."

Chapter Nine

Cal Morgan inspected the mechanism of the ladder. After the flat numbing shock of unbelief that he could be so intent on the money as to allow himself to be sealed in a room beyond help, he had talked himself into a temporary calm. Nothing was ever so complicated as it looked. He had a basic knowledge of mechanics and there would be a simple way out if you kept control. It was not quite four and he should be able to come up with the answer in less than an hour. Then, at worst, he would find Madge awake. Whatever excuse he could make, she would probably catch on and that would be the end of this approach. But her fear of Driscoll alone would keep her from giving him away. It would be very bad but not entirely over. On the other hand, if Driscoll caught him in that room — God! He would have to hurry. Yet, he must not hurry his thinking.

The ladder was quite easy to understand. It was not the magic it appeared to be. As he suspected, it ran on steel tracks that came down from the slot in the ceiling to the floor. The tracks gave it solidity and direction. Also it was raised and lowered by a thick cable which must wind on a drum. It would be something like the operation of a winch, hoisting an anchor. Then when the ladder cleared the floor opening, it would trip switch that would close the sliding door. He understood all that perfectly. It was an obvious deduction from what could be seen. But the problem lay in what could not be seen. And that was the drum and the motor which turned it. From the sound, it must be above the ceiling in some small space. But when he climbed the ladder he could find no access to that space whatsoever. And even if he could find the motor, that was no guarantee he could make it work.

He came down and went over the room for the second time with still greater care. There wasn't a hint of anything, even on the steel panels of the safe, like a button, lever or switch. He made still another search, combing the walls, floor and ceiling with microscopic deliberateness. Nothing. That was when he felt panic.

Still he forced consequences from his mind. You could not think in cluttered terms of the dangerous future. There was only now. He squatted in front of the safe and began to study the dial. This was a four-tumbler job with numbers from zero to ninety-nine.

He knew that his chances of coming up with the

right numbers were literally a million to one. And outside of fictional safe crackers, no one could twist that
dial and feel out the combination. Yet there might be
more than money in that safe. There might be a clue to
the way out. The only clue. It could even be possible that
the opening of this door tripped a switch that opened
the other.

He remembered now why he had been fairly confi-
dent that he would open the safe if there was one in the
room. It went back to those numbers — three-nine-five-
four. Driscoll was a man of unusual consistency. If for
some sentimental or other reason he used those numbers
twice, he would be likely to use them again. Cal Morgan
began to twirl the dial, spinning it clear, then picking
up the number three right, making three turns left to
nine, two right to five and one left to four. The sequence
of turns was standard-four, three, two, one, though the
alternation of lefts and rights was conjecture.

Now he pushed down on the door handle. It refused
entrance. Not discouraged, he tried again, this time
spinning right where he had spun left. That didn't work
either. So he tried the numbers backward with the same
result. He had been wrong after all.

He looked at his watch. Twenty-eight minutes after
four. He could feel the pressure building inside him like
lidded steam. Moisture was on his brow and there was
an unpleasant clamminess under his arms. His whole
life was a thing of closed doors. He looked around him
and had the uneasy feeling of chest expansion, like
holding your breath underwater. He wondered if in time
the air in that room would be exhausted.

The room had been provided with an overhead light
that went on the minute the sliding door opened and
must stay on until you went down the ladder and it came
up empty.

But looking around he could see no vent for air. Either air came from the slot that received the ladder above him, or there was none. That is, there were so many cubic feet of air, but unless there was a vent, it would be used up in a certain number of hours. Much would depend on his being calm. Heavy breathing, exertion, would multiply the usage of oxygen.

Yet how could he be calm? The damn room was a trap. He would either be discovered or, in time, he would suffocate.

Think. Think!

He began to concentrate on the numbers of the dial.

After a time it came to him that Driscoll had probably used a more complicated arrangement of the numbers. Why should he waste ninety per cent of the dial by sticking to numbers below ten? Perhaps he had used thirty-nine, fifty-four, then gone back to a three and a nine. He tried the sequence quickly, running through it twice with alternate turns. The safe door held.

Now again he looked at his watch. It was twenty-one minutes before five. He had that frantic feeling of the end of a terrible gamble. The wrong end. Driscoll must be already arranging his affairs, cleaning up the last details to come home. Driscoll would discover him there and Driscoll would be armed. Or worse, he would be undiscovered too long. And Madge would be wide-awake, angry in the thought that he had crept away in such a hurry that he had left some of his clothes. She might be pacing the living room now. Then, seeing him come up from the basement, it would be all over.

You played against trouble, forgetting that trouble held aces, too. And wore a poker face of danger.

Desperately, he tried another run of numbers — thirty-nine, fifty-four, then reverse-fifty-four, thirty-nine. Nothing there, either. He ran it again, changing direction of turns. He pushed down on the handle. It held fast.

Well, there was that dirty little box that Barney had brought for Driscoll. If it worked, and there was always a chance that it wouldn't, Driscoll would be delayed. It was even possible that out of fear, he could kill himself. But if so, it would be a long time before Madge would get into this room. And by then . . .

That kind of thinking was fruitless. The dial. The dial! Not even the money interested him now. The thing was to get out. And if the panel had no control in the room, it must open with the safe. If he could get the safe open, he would lick the whole problem.

But, God almighty, he had tried everything. There was no point in fooling with the damn dial willy-nilly. He had to think the way Driscoll would think when he planned that combination. Because Driscoll managed anything he touched. He wouldn't just take factory numbers. He would have his own. And they would have meaning.

Now he began to go over everything Madge had ever told him about Driscoll pertaining to the safe and especially his hoarding of the money.

There was something there that she had told him during that period right after he had begun the affair with her. Something solid and applicable. But so long ago.

He kept reaching back, hearing her conversation. But it wouldn't come to him. And then he caught a fragment . . .

". . . And Greg has this crazy idea, this senseless goal. He wants to save this great cache of money, I don't know how much, and he's set himself a time limit to do it."

A time limit, thought Cal. But how much time? How

much time, Madge?

". . . He said it was going to take a long time but he would positively do it in . . . in . . ."

Yes?

"In fifteen years."

Fifteen years, thought Cal. Then would fifteen be a key number? No. That doesn't hold up. But suppose-suppose you took the year he began and the year he should end? And put them together. Wouldn't that be just the way he would come up with a combination? Sure. Real meaning there.

Let's see — take the numbers you have, thirty-nine, fiftyfour. You subtract one from the other and you get — of course! Fifteen. So what's missing? Nineteen. And that must be the key number. Nineteen thirty-nine to nineteen fifty-four.

God! It has to be right.

He cleared the dial, then ran through the turns, using nineteen, thirty-nine, then nineteen again and fifty-four.

It didn't work, so he tried again reversing the direction.

He pushed down on the handle. It gave easily. He heaved a great sigh of relief.

He pulled. The door swung open.

He saw the great orderly stacks of banded bills. But he wasn't really looking. He was watching the panel.

It remained closed.

It was a gruesome joke.

All that money and no way out.

He peered around the bins inside the safe. He couldn't see any kind of switch. Anyway, there wasn't enough light.

He stayed very still for a moment. He washed his hands together as if this would quiet their trembling.

Then he began to run his palms over the walls of the safe. Nothing there.

He tried the ceiling surface, reaching back and working forward. He came to the leading edge and, at this point, he felt a small rough spot against the heel of his palm.

He ducked in and looked up. He smiled. Almost flush with the surface there was a tiny red button. He pressed it. Then wished he hadn't. Why was it red? A signal?

But when he turned, the panel was sliding open. The light flashed on below. With the whine of that distant motor, the ladder descended. He looked at his watch. It was quarter of five. At least he would be spared the sealed room. And Driscoll. He made a swift appraisal of the money.

The bills were in denominations of hundreds and fifties. Some were new. Most were old. He picked up a banded suck of hundreds and made an estimate. It looked like a hundred bills to the stack. That meant he held in his hand ten thousand dollars! And all of the wrappers seemed, to contain the same amount of bills. In that case — a half million? Probably more. He had never seen that much money. How could he know?

He looked at the money and thought of its power. He came to a decision. There was just the smallest chance . . .

He tossed the ten thousand dollar stack on top and, leaving the safe open, stepped down the ladder so fast he fell at the bottom, recovered and swept out of the room to bound up the cellar stairs on the balls of his feet.

He paused in the kitchen and listened. He could hear nothing but the faint whir of the big refrigerator.

Suppose Driscoll wasn't delayed? Suppose he came home early? Suppose Madge. . . ? The hell with it!

He tiptoed into the living room. No sign of her.

Still on the balls of his feet, he crept up to the stairs, paused at the top landing, listened, went on.

The bedroom door was ajar as he had left it. He peeked in. Madge had turned in sleep toward the wall. But she was *still* asleep. Oh, God, what luck!

Back down the stairs, out to the garage, lifting the door, opening the trunk of his car, grabbing the burlap bags he had brought just in case. He left the trunk open. Likewise the garage door.

He gulped air to ease the tension, meanwhile looking around the house and grounds, down the sweep of lawn to the street. All was still, nothing move neighboring houses too far removed and screened by trees for visibility.

He went into the house the way he had just now left it, by the back door. Down to the cellar and up to the safe. Madly, he filled the sacks, wiped fingerprints from the safe walls with a handkerchief, closed the door, wiped the handle.

Down below he jumped off the ladder, then when it didn't ascend, put weight on the bottom rung until it did.

He climbed under the bench, closed the alarm switch and workroom door. Then he went out to the garage with the sacks.

Back in Madge's room he tore out of his clothes in a frenzy of haste, eased over so gently onto the bed, pulling the sheet over him. He looked at the clock on the nightstand. It was two minutes after five.

Now he shook Madge roughly by the shoulder. "Madge. Madge! Wake up! It's after five. Quick! Get dressed. Hurry!"

She came awake wide-eyed. Startled. Frightened.

"What time is it?" she said. "What time is it!"

"I told you. After five. I don't know how it happened. I just lay back for a moment and then I was asleep. When I woke up just now, it was . . ."

"Oh, Lord. Lord! Don't talk," she said. "Just hurry. Get dressed!"

Once more he shoved into his clothes, this time from underwear out. There was only a moment to enjoy, from the corner of his eye, the lithe swing of her body out of bed, the profile bounce of her breasts. Her body disappeared into panty and bra, the dress came down over her head. She was racing a comb through her hair as he pulled on his coat.

"How about tomorrow?" He said breathlessly.

"No!" she said. "We're leaving in the afternoon for Cumberland Lake. For the weekend. We have a place there. Call me Monday. Will you be in town?"

"For at least another week. I'll make it longer."

"Falling asleep was suicide," she muttered, finishing with her hair and lipstick, looking crisp as ever. "He'll be home in minutes," she said. "Go. Run!"

He kissed her cheek so as not to spoil her make-up. "Monday," he said.

He plunged down the stairs and out of the house. He backed and turned recklessly, racing down the drive, leaving the garage door open as before. He saw her at the window as he fled past, waved but didn't wait to see if she responded.

He had gone perhaps two miles when just ahead he saw that there had been an accident. To his left, a small knot of people were gathered around an automobile that had smashed into a tree. A man was trudging away from the scene toward Cal. The way he walked, looking straight ahead, half stumbling, he appeared to be in a state of shock. And now a woman from the group around the car was pointing at him.

The man was walking on the other side of the road and when Cal came almost abreast of him, he slowed and turned for a good look.

He was quite sure. It was Driscoll, the good Captain, looking anything but proud and in command, his clothing disarrayed, pain on his face.

Cal pressed down on the accelerator. His features relaxed into a slow, smug grin.

Chapter Ten

After Barney left him alone again, Brick got up and took a cold shower, then stretched out on the bed and began to read the paper. He felt good — for about ten minutes. Then he was in another sweat. Angrily he tossed the paper on the floor and let his thoughts drift back to Driscoll.

There was a certain twisted pleasure in remembering the worst of it, the part that came after their arrest. Because now time had run out for Driscoll and this was Brick's golden hour. And in remembering, he renewed his hate.

*T*he truck slowed, came to a grinding halt before the dark buildings of Company "B."

The sergeant vaulted over the tailgate to the ground, lowered the gate and said, "LaMatta, Olson, Carmedy and Goldstein — bring the prisoners. The rest of you, stay put." Four MPs dismounted with their captives. "Which way is your Orderly Room?" the sergeant said.

"That building over there," Brick said, pointing.

"I'll send your CQ for the Captain," said the sergeant. "He's not going to be happy. He's probably in the sack."

The group moved in loose formation toward the Orderly Room, from which came a dim light. At that very moment, an officer stepped from the building and approached. He was in full uniform and wore sidearms. Brick saw immediately that it was Captain Driscoll.

It was not unusual for the Captain to be abroad so late. It was his custom, once or twice a week, to check the guard posts personally.

"That's Captain Driscoll now," murmured Brick to the sergeant. "Must have heard the truck."

"Halt!" the sergeant said to the detail. He stood at attention until the officer was a few feet away, then saluted sharply. Driscoll returned the salute just as sharply, coming to a halt in front of the sergeant.

"Trouble, Sergeant?" the Captain said. He squinted in amazement at the three civilians, recognition coming slowly to his face. "Let's see — Hambrick, Morgan, and Sykes. Almost three days overdue from passes. Bad business. These men were on orders for overseas shipment. Wearing civilian clothes, especially at this time, constitutes intent to desert."

"Yes, sir," said the sergeant. "We picked them up at the railroad depot in San Francisco. And I thought, sir, that the Captain might . . ."

"Bring these men where we can have a look at them, Sergeant," Driscoll said. "Just follow me."

Driscoll led the way to a mess hall, mounted steps, opened a door and turned on lights. The prisoners and their guards followed. The Captain closed the door, took a seat center of one of the mess tables and waited while the group gathered, standing at attention opposite him, MPs flanking the prisoners. The Captain looked at each of the prisoners in turn. His eyes held on the face of Cal Morgan for a long, painful moment. The silence was profound.

"At ease," he said then. "Now, Sergeant, let me have your report."

The sergeant cleared his throat. "Well, sir, my detail was makin' a check of the depot. We picked up a drunk and then I spotted this one . . .." he indicate Barney ". . . about to hop a train for New York. He was wearin' these clothes but he had on an army belt and he didn't look right to me. GI haircut and he talked and acted like a soldier. I nailed him and when I see he was with the others, I nailed them, too. These men had passes in their wallets but their leave was up Wednesday reveille. They admitted they were tryin' to grab that train, so I brought them all in. That's about it, sir. Here's the train tickets I took off them."

Driscoll inspected the tickets.

"Very good, Sergeant. Why didn't you confine these men in the post stockade and make your report to me in the morning?"

"Well, sir, I'll tell you. These men are not stateside goldbricks. They're fresh from overseas. They're combat troops. And from the story they tell, they ve had a rough go of it, being shipped right out again. I like to give men like these every break."

"That is not a decision for you to make, Sergeant,"

Driscoll said firmly. "These men should have embarked this morning. They were attempting to escape hazardous duty."

"Yes, sir," the sergeant said. "Beg-pardon, sir, but has the Captain fought with the troops? Does the Captain know what this can do to a man?"

"I consider that an insolent question, Sergeant. And insubordinate."

"Yes, sir. Sorry, sir. I just thought perhaps the Captain had a certain, uh — feeling for his own men. Does the Captain wish us to remain or would he like to talk to the prisoners in private?"

"Please, Captain Driscoll," said Brick. "We'd like to have a word with you alone. It won't take a minute."

Driscoll scratched his nose with a forefinger, studying Brick thoughtfully. Again his eyes drifted to Cal Morgan, briefly, but with an odd look of speculation. Morgan shifted uneasily and the Captain looked back to Brick. He sighed. His face sagged into weary lines. "All right," he said. "I'll talk to you men in private."

"Thank you, sir," said Brick. "If the Captain will just listen to our side of it."

Driscoll looked again at the tickets. "One way to New York," he said. "You would have some kind of a case if you had bought round-trip tickets." He shook his head. "But this is bad. What's in those bags?"

"Our uniforms," said Brick.

"I see," said Driscoll, frowning. "Sergeant, take your men and wait outside the door until I call you."

The sergeant saluted and departed with his men.

When the door closed, Brick relaxed. He produced a pack of cigarettes, lighted one and put his foot up on the bench of the mess hall table. Jets of smoke came from his nostrils as he leaned toward Captain Driscoll, said, "Now! We can talk."

Driscoll looked at him with unbelief. "At ease doesn't mean slouch, Sergeant Hambrick. We haven't dispensed with regulations. And did I say you could smoke?"

"All right, look, Captain. Let's take it for granted that I respect you as an officer of the United States Army and all that stuff. But what I have to say can't be said with all that third person formality crap. It would take a month. I'd a like permission to come out from behind the army double-talk and speak like men. Are you willing to speak to me like a man for about five minutes, Captain?"

Driscoll smiled faintly. He nodded assent. "It's not the army way," he said. "But I realize these are serious charges and I want you to have every reasonable chance. You may all smoke and you may speak freely." Once more he shifted his gaze to Morgan, then Sykes and back to Brick.

Brick sucked in a deep breath, "Captain, I'm going to appeal to you as a man of reason and intelligence. I'm going to start right out by admitting that what we were attempting to do was wrong, in the eyes of the government. But as a man, suppose I promised that after risking your life three times to defend me, you could return to be with your wife for a period of time? And then sent you right back, without so much as a look at your family, to risk your life again in a hell from which you were pretty goddamn sure you'd never return. Wouldn't you hate me? Wouldn't you walk out on me? Be honest now. Not as an officer, but as a man!"

"You know, Hambrick," Driscoll said. "I'm really disappointed. I had hoped that you had some private information, some circumstance that would help reduce the charges against you men. Because I tell you frankly that in time of war you couldn't get into a more serious jam.

"But for the sake of argument, let's see how a government at war would look at your assertion that you have been unfairly treated. In the first place you don't seem to understand that there is nothing fair about war at all. War is a brutal, death struggle for the survival of a country and its freedom. Until it's over, there can be no fair play for individuals. Or, if those are just words to you, put it this way. Is it fair that while you are alive and safe, many of your buddies have been, and are right now being, killed or wounded in action? No. And you speak of promises. There are no promises in war, as such. There is only luck. Occasionally a little luck for a few. If a combat soldier happens to be in the States and the army can spare him for a time, he gets a furlough. That is not a promise. Because the minute the situation changes, the minute there is an offensive in which a trained soldier is needed, the furlough order is rescinded. Why? Because the fight must come first, or the whole war effort would fall apart and you wouldn't have any country left to give you fair play. No, I'm sorry. The fact that you men think you have been unfairly treated is no excuse for attempting desertion."

"Crap!" said Brick, bringing his fist down on the table. "You're talking like a goddamn GI manual. Don't talk to me about individuals. What about the hundred and fifty million individuals who never fired a gun at anything more dangerous than a moose in their whole lives? And never will. Why, for God's sake, you've never so much as heard the sound of enemy guns. How do you know you wouldn't run and hide like a gopher the first shot fired in your direction?"

"It's not my fault, Sergeant, that I haven't had a chance to find out. God knows, I've applied for transfer to a combat unit often enough. And though I doubt it, I might just run and hide. But my personal behavior at some future time has nothing to do with your situation now."

"Crap!" said Brick. "Give you just a couple of days on the line and I'll bet we could talk man to man. Don't you think you might have reacted the same way in our places? Give me just one honest answer."

Driscoll considered, drumming his fingers on the table. "I think not," he said. "We're made of different stuff. We look at the war from different standpoints. In your code, there is no sacrifice, only personal advantage. Still, anything is possible —"

"There!" said Brick. It's possible! So give us a break. Write the whole thing off as AWOL — an overstay of pass. But you don't have to wreck us with a desertion charge. That ship is still loading. You could send us down in a jeep and no one would be the wiser. Have a heart, Captain. The MP sergeant will cooperate. And you have the power to gloss the whole thing over, don't you?"

Driscoll pushed back his chair, stood. He walked across the room to a window. Hands clenched behind his back, he peered into the night. When he turned, his face looked drawn, old. He sighed.

"You make it sound easy," he said. "It isn't. There never was a more difficult decision to make. I wish at this moment I could turn the whole thing over to a senior officer in this command. Have it off my conscience. Because apart from right and wrong, I see clearly that you have served better and suffered more than I have, than millions of others. In peacetime there would be no doubt in my mind. There would be plenty of room for, as you say, having a heart. And I would let you go with company punishment." He crossed the room, sat down again.

"But now to answer your question, yes, I could probably get you on that troop ship. And you may not ever believe this, yet that would be the easiest way out for me. But I can't do it. For the good of the service, for the good of the other men in this company, I can't do it."

"Why?" said Morgan. "Why the hell can't you do it, Captain?"

Driscoll looked at Morgan and the first real anger crept into his face. His mouth opened, then clamped shut. He seemed to be controlling himself with great difficulty.

"There ain't no way he can't do it," said Barney. "He means he won't."

"Yes," said Driscoll, "I mean that, too. I won't. I certainly won't. But I'll tell you why. Because it would undermine discipline. An army without discipline is no army. It's a mob out of control. Don't you think there are others in this company who would take off for the hills if they thought they could get away with it? There are men out there in the company street who are scared. They don't want to fight and they know they are going to have to. They want to see their families and they can't. But if they thought they faced nothing but an AWOL charge or company punishment, they would scatter like milkweed in the wind. Tonight, they would most all be gone. And they know. Don't think they don't. They know you missed the convoy to the boat. The word came back to me from the First Sergeant. They're convinced you deserted. And git away with it. There's your answer. There's your why and your won't. I despise what you did. But I'm sorry for you."

"Yeah, Captain," said Brick. "We know how sorry you are."

"Anyone have anything else to add?" asked Driscoll. "Sykes?"

"Nothin'. Except you're a — Nothin'. I have nothin' to say."

"Morgan?"

"What could I say to you?" said Cal. "We live in different worlds. And there's no communication between."

Driscoll ran his eyes over Morgan from head to toe. He seemed about to say something. Instead he stood up. He looked at his watch. "That's all then," he said. "I have to check the guard." He began to walk across the room to the door.

"Hold it, Captain!" Brick's voice was like a shot in the room. Driscoll turned.

"Well," he said.

Brick moved toward dim, a frantic look on his face. "You haven't told us what you're gonna do."

"I'm going to charge each of you with attempting willful, premeditated desertion," said Driscoll, "and attempting to escape hazardous duty. As of this moment, you are under arrest and will be placed in the post stockade until trial by a General Court." He turned again to the door.

"Wait!" Brick caught him by the arm and swung him around.

"Take your hands off me, Hambrick," said Driscoll.

"I'll make a bargain with you, Captain," said Brick. "Let these two go and I'll take the whole rap. I planned it. I talked them into it."

"Never," said Driscoll. "Do you murder a man because someone else suggests it? You're all equally guilty. Now, I'm through —"

"All right, you dirty, squealing sonofabitch," Brick said hoarsely through clenched teeth. "But you're not gonna get out of this room until you show how much of a man you are. Unless you are a man, you're not gonna get out of this room alive." He gave Driscoll a shove away from the door.

"I'm warning you, Hambrick," said Driscoll. With a quick upward movement of his hand, he lifted the flap of his holster and the big service .45 appeared in his fist. Immediately, the great bear arms of Barney Sykes closed around him from behind and forced the gun arm down. With a quick wrench, Brick tore the gun from his grasp, reversed it and jammed it hard against his mouth so that a thin stream of blood trickled down Driscoll's chin from his lip.

"One word," said Brick, pulling back the hammer, "Just one sound out of you to call the guard, and I'll blow the back of your head off through your goddamn squealing mouth. We got nothin' to lose. Nod your head if you don't want it blown off."

Driscoll nodded under the pressure of the barrel. Brick removed the .45 and stepped back. Driscoll wiped his mouth, smearing blood on the back of his hand.

"All right," said Brick, passing the gun to Barney. "Take off the rank, Driscoll. Peel off that jacket. And don't be afraid, you big tin god. No one's gonna touch you but me."

Driscoll stood blinking at Brick, blood still coursing down his chin from the cut in his lip.

Brick stepped closer. "Let's see what a man you are," he said. "Let's see you behave in the gallant tradition of the army. Take off that jacket and fight!"

Slowly Driscoll unbuttoned his jacket with the silver bars of his rank, tossed it on the table, removed his shirt. He stood in his undershirt, narrow-chested, but surprisingly muscular and hard of bicep.

Barney pushed Driscoll to the center of the room. "Kill him, Brick," he said. "Murder the bastard! If you don't, I will.''

Driscoll assumed a fighter's stance, guard up. He looked like a man who knew he was fighting for his life and was determined to do so bravely. Brick approached him with a killer's smile, but with his arms at his side. Driscoll slammed a piston left that connected with Brick's jaw, rocking his head back.

"Good boy!" said Brick, moving in again. "I love you for that, you poor tin slob. You may be half a man after all.''

Driscoll swung a long right, but Brick ducked neatly and slapped him a powerful blow across the face with his open hand. Crack! It sent Driscoll reeling sideways. Brick laughed. Then his face went blank and a new look came into his eyes. His big fists balled, one arm shot out and delivered a bone crushing blow to the side of Driscoll's head. Driscoll's eyes glazed, he shook his head and, ducking under, caught Brick in the stomach. Brick chopped downward and splintered Driscoll's nose with one great blow, rammed two teeth back into his mouth with the next, and as Driscoll toppled backward, missed his chin and nearly crushed his adam's apple.

Now Brick bent over and hauled Driscoll up by his belt. Driscoll's head lolled. Brick pulled his arm back for a blow that would have caved in Driscoll's face. But at that moment, the door burst open and the sergeant of MPs shouted "Hold it! That's enough!" The sergeant leveled a submachine gun, two other MPs held cocked .45's. "Climb off of him. Quick!" he said to Brick. "And you there, drop that pistol or I'll cut you in half.'' Barney let the gun fall with a clatter.

"Now," the sergeant said, "let's take a ride to the guard house. You guys have had it.''

At the trial they were defended by a clever lawyer from New York, a former officer of their old division.

This officer enlarged upon their bravery in action, their previous good conduct and their long absence from the United States in three nerve-shattering campaigns. The defense further pointed out that there was no proof of desertion nor its intent, since after all, the defendants might readily have returned after a brief visit with their families. The defense concluded with a statement that no charge could be reasonably upheld but that of absence without leave.

On the other hand, the prosecution observed that the defendants had every intention to desert. They ware civilian clothes. They had one way tickets to New York, although they had the funds for a round-trip each. And further, New York was not the residence of all, but only of Sergeant Hambrick. So how could it be assumed that they were merely returning home for a short leave? And, above all, had they not been apprehended, they could not have returned in time for movement with a newly assigned unit being shipped to a combat area overseas. To miss or avoid a troop movement constituted the clearest evidence of desertion and also an attempt to escape hazardous duty.

Driscoll, his face still slightly bruised and swollen, had been a rather reluctant witness for the prosecution. In view of the beating he took, he was surprisingly human. He refused to allow an additional charge of assaulting an officer, resisting arrest, and so on. It was later said of his testimony (though not by Brick, Cal, or Barney) that it was impartial, just. He was aware of the hardships these men had endured, their need to go home. But he was still more aware of the army's need to maintain discipline. He emphatically did not believe the trio attempted desertion because of cowardice.

But after a short deliberation, the court-martial passed upon Brick, Cal, and Barney for their try at desertion and their attempt to escape hazardous duty, life sentences, the sentences to be carried out in the federal prison at Leavenworth — each to be dishonorably discharged from the service.

The three men were transported to Leavenworth. Doors closed. And locked. A final sound. Names became numbers. They were forgotten.

But didn't forget.

Under the caution of Brick, they were well behaved. Ironically, a few months after their imprisonment, the war ended. The battle cries, the fever of patriotism, the condemnation of non-patriots died.

There were amnesties. Sentences were reduced. Those of Brick, Barney, and Cal were cut to twelve years.

But those twelve years were an eternity of despair.

Brick thought now about how this prison life had crushed his spirit, wiped out the better part of his youth, taken his home, his business, his wife. He relived the midnight mess hall betrayal of Driscoll as he had a hundred times. With terrible hate, he thought how easy it would have been for Driscoll to save them with a word to the sergeant, "Release these men in my custody, Sergeant. They're good men and I'll back them if anything comes of it." And there it would have ended. But no, the cold-blooded bastard wasn't satisfied. Not until he had destroyed them. And now Driscoll, having long forgotten in the ease and splendor of his life, would pay the big price. Brick would see to it.

Brick heard voices. In a moment Barney exploded into the room shouting, "He's here! Cal's here! And he's got it. The sonofabitch did it. He's got the money!"

Brick sat up abruptly as Cal, carrying two giant burlap bags, entered behind Barney.

Fascinated, Brick watched as Cal set the bags on the bed. One toppled over and spilled green stacks of hundred-dollar bibs.

"God Almighty!" said Brick. "Now we can buy the world. The whole god damned world!"

Chapter Eleven

A few minutes after five that afternoon, Gregory Driscoll was on his way home, moving without haste through the tight pockets of anxious commuters, the twisting snarl of vehicles scurrying for position. Oblivious of the struggle, Driscoll listened as usual to the five o'clock news, pacing himself so that he would hit the lights just as they flashed green.

Not given to the emotional extremes of soaring elation or plunging melancholy, he nevertheless was in quite decent spirits. Even the ninety-degree heat was a minor irritation. For tomorrow there would be the grand weekend at Cumberland Lake, cool in the tree-shadowed cliffside house, below which were his private dock and boat shed with its forty-foot cruiser, the Chris Craft speedboat and outboard launch. There would be the bland, gray shimmer of the morning lake, the misty silence of dawn fishing, the noonday dip with the clean chillness of the water washing him with peace and remoteness. And especially there would be Madge.

Somehow they were always closer at the small house by the lake. The servants were left behind, Bobbie was at camp in the Adirondacks, and they were entirely alone. Madge was more restful and relaxed, they seemed to communicate on a deeper level, without the usual remoteness.

In fact, he had just about come to the conclusion that if she was responsive during the coming weekend, he was going to have a serious talk with her. There were barriers which had stood between them too long, barriers which would never come down without an attempt at total honesty.

Yet, every time he came even close to honesty with her, he had checked himself in time. Because while truth might bridge the gap between them, there was even a better chance that it might separate them completely, irrevocably.

Still, if it was true that time softened even the grimmest tragedy, altered the viewpoint, time was in his favor. He could probe around the edges of the thing and see how Madge reacted. He could always retreat as he had so many times. And in any case, it was going to be a good weekend.

Even so, there was that uncomfortable feeling, however recessed, of something out of shape in the pattern of his life. The sly cruelty of the Buick rigged, the utilities ordered off the three a.m. phone call, was still a boil festering in his mind. Like dark clouds in the distance of a clear sky, there was the threat of trouble. So that, remembering, he had inspected the Buick this time, lifting the hood, peering underneath, circling from bumper to bumper. Everything had appeared in order. Perhaps, after all, it was a minor flurry of hate, quickly spent.

The news over, the weather report delivered, he

switched off the radio and sank back against the seat, the traffic thinning as he came now to the tree-lined green suburb of his orbit.

It was after he had passed the last stoplight before a rather long open stretch of hillside mansions which peered below with cloistered dignity from behind tall clusters of trees, that he had the sneaking awareness of a stealthy presence there with him in the car. The feeling came and went like some weak pulse of warning in the background of his thoughts. Since it was not a conscious knowing, but rather as subtle as intuition, he paid no attention to it. At first.

But then he caught from the corner of his eye a quick, darting movement at the back edge of his right shoulder. Then motionless waiting, with the cunning shadow of the thing still held in image.

He was frightened. Perhaps more frightened than he could ever remember. And in the substrata of thought, he knew why. And supressed the knowledge. Because he dared not look at it. To drift around the edge of possibility was one thing. But to know was panic. Yet he had to know.

He gave one last glance to the road, lifted his foot from the accelerator and with an agony of control, slowly turned his head. At that precise moment, the thing which he had partly seen came with a dark hoisting and crawling over the back edge of the seat and paused, seemingly to confront him.

What he saw was a spider. No ordinary spider. But such a gigantic exaggeration of the crafty little insects of his knowledge, that it could have crawled from some science fiction nightmare.

This one that squatted now on the top edge of his seat with a look of crouched, diabolical waiting, rested on eight darkly hairy legs longer than a man's fingers and had an oblong body the size of a man's fist or a small crab. The hairs on the legs seemed to bristle with electrical tension sent from the dark gray mass of loathsome body.

Though Driscoll did not know it, this was a giant tarantula of a species known to entomologists as a Bird spider. Driscoll knew only that it *was* a spider, venomous, grotesque, unthinkably large. And since one of Driscoll's secret fears was of any kind of spider at all, he did not need to be bitten. He was already paralyzed.

There had been a time when a black spider not a third the size of this tarantula had crawled up his trouser leg. And he had run, twisting and turning and clawing at himself. And, to his anguish, had been seen. He was then a captain in the army and it had happened on the drill field during a ten minute break. He had been sitting on the ground, he had felt this thing, saw it going up his leg, had leaped up and gone through such gymnastics, pulling down his pants and brushing the spider to earth, that his own men had seen. And known. And turned away with sly smiles. Yet, in greater things, in the area of the known, you could not find a braver man than Gregory Driscoll.

Now as he sat staring at the spider, Driscoll saw for himself the most ridiculous and loathsome of ends. He did not know that this huge tarantula, though poisonous, would inflict a bite far less deadly than the comparatively tiny Black Widow. Yet because fear is the most deadly of poisons, a woman in a remote section of California had died from heart failure caused by the shock of seeing just such a spider crawl toward her over the coverlet of her bed.

Without taking his eyes from the spider, which now seemed to shuffle its legs, then crouch to spring, Driscoll pressed down on the brake and slowly came to a stop.

With a mighty effort to keep from exciting the spider to action, his mouth hanging open, he held back the sudden need for a sobbing intake of breath.

Slowly he reached his hand for the door handle and lifted. When the latch gave, he shoved out with one great tortured leap, slammed the door and ran gasping to the rear of the car. Here, as gawking drivers streamed by, he leaned on the deck of the trunk and waited for the convulsion of trembling to subside.

The absurd thing was that he needed help, could not go on with the spider in the car, but on the other hand, could not ask for that help. How could you stop one of those passing cars, say, "Please come help me kill a spider," and still remain the shadow of a man? So, in the end, he found a long, flat board and with sweating courage, flattened the spider where it leered from the seat he had just left. He swept the revolting thing out the door and, sick enough to vomit, got back in the car and drove away.

He had gone about a mile when he was electrified by the same sort of insidious awareness of a filthy presence. This time he met it quite directly by lifting his head and eyes to the headliner above him. The tarantula that hung just over him was, if anything, larger, and from this view, twice as terrifying, with the whole mass of its hairy body exposed downward. And this time a wild sound did come out of Driscoll's throat, and he jammed the brakes too hard, jerking the car. The spider fell. It landed writhing to his forehead and bounced to his lap. That was when he gave the wheel an involuntary wrench and careened off the road into a tree.

Chapter Twelve

*T*he front end of the car was demolished. But strangely Driscoll was merely shaken. Yet, if he had broken a leg, he would have hurled himself from the car with the same speed as he did the moment he recovered from the shock of the crash.

As he jumped from the car, the spider fell to the ground and scurried away in ugly confusion. Unmindful of the accident, Driscoll moved dazedly off, feeling the place on his head where the dirty thing had touched. Though he was sure he had been bitten, he could find no mark or swelling. He supposed that it had happened too fast for the spider to get a purchase. Relieved, he still could not control the trembling of his limbs as he continued on down the road.

By now, several cars had pulled off the highway and a small knot of people had gathered at the scene of the accident, some milling about the car, others watching him in amazement as he walked away.

Driscoll did not want to go back to the car. He did not ever want to set eyes on it again. Even if the car were taken apart piece by piece, fumigated, any remaining spiders exterminated, he would never be able to sit in it again without the sensation of something crawling over his flesh, or at least a stealthy creeping behind him. And how impossible it would be to ever use the car at night!

No, in the morning he would arrange to have delivered a shiny Cadillac right from the showroom floor. It was near to the change of models, it was a buyer's market, and this could easily be arranged. It was only because of his inate frugality and simplicity of taste that he had not bought a Cadillac long ago.

After a good fifteen minutes, during which he had no sense of time, the heat, or the exertion of walking, he came to a small shopping center. He entered a drugstore and placed a call to an automobile association all-night garage. He gave the location of the wreck and ordered it towed away and repaired. His insurance company would take care of all but the fifty dollars deductible. He instructed that a taxi be sent to his home with the briefcase he had left on the front seat. Then, as an afterthought, he warned that the wrecking crew be on the lookout for one or more large, deadly spiders which might be lurking in the car. He wasn't surprised when the garage man acted as though he wasn't quite right. At least, in all good conscience, he had done his best.

Now he thought of calling Madge and asking her to come down and pick him up in the Thunderbird. He decided against it. He wasn't ready to explain the accident. He had to think about it. The only explanation he had ready at the moment might make him appear ridiculous.

He called a taxi company and was told it would be at least twenty minutes before they could send him a cab. He said that was perfectly all right. He would wait.

He sat down in a booth and ordered coffee. He began to feel the first soreness of muscle, the ache of legs and arms caused by the jolt. He dismissed it as unimportant and began a thoughtful contemplation of the whole problem.

Although even this was painful, he began to go over

every scrap of information he had ever gleaned about spiders. He was not well versed on the subject only because it had been too repugnant to arouse his curiosity.

But in the end, he came up at last with the memory of one of those short subject films about wildlife which included insects. It was an old Disney thing taken on the desert and there had been some nauseous shots of spiders of a large variety. The name finally came to him — tarantula! The very sound of it was venomous. Tarantula. But that was it. He was quite certain.

He could not be sure, but it seemed logical that such a spider would not normally be found iii this part of the country. They probably came from desert places, California, perhaps Florida or South America. He would inquire. But even if you admitted that such spiders existed in Kentucky, they wouldn't be crawling around a parking lot but in some woods or swampland. But stretch the imagination. Say one did by some freak of circumstance make its way into his car. One, yes. But hardly two. And there probably had been more.

So he could only come to the conclusion that the spiders had been turned loose in his car by some person with a consuming hatred. Certainly the same person or persons who began by tampering with thc Buick. And it was no longer the work of some twisted crank. The spiders had probably been brought from another state or imported from another country by someone who meant to kill him. This was a damn serious, frightening business.

Well, he had friends in the police department. He knew Gibson, the chief, and Kelly, the night supervisor. But for that very reason, he was unwilling to ask for help. He had joined the National Guard, had risen to full colonel and was respected as a man of courage and resourcefulness, a man who handled his own affairs in the most disciplined and fearless manner. How would it look if he said, "Listen, Gibson, I want you to send around a couple of your boys. You see, I've been set upon by spiders, and someone has tampered with my car." He might get a grudging action, but never again respect with this statement from a leader in business, a colonel in the Guard. No, the last resort would be to call the police.

Chapter Thirteen

*H*e had thought about it before, and now he thought about it again. There was absolutely no one, man or woman, who had real cause to hate him. He had always, to the best of his knowledge, been fair in his business dealings. He hadn't taken advantage of anyone in trade, purchase, or sale. He didn't want to, he didn't have to.

He was good to his employees, working then a five day week, providing up to three weeks vacation and paying salaries well above the average scale for Louise. For this very reason, he had a small turnover through the years and most who worked for him were intensely loyal.

Occasionally it was necessary to discharge an employee for just cause. But, though his people were fired by department heads, he personally investigated every case to be sure there was no bias, often encouraging his executives to give an employee who faltered a second and even a third chance where there were family and other personal problems involved.

Anyway, it had been over a year since anyone had left his employ with a dismissal. No, nothing there at all.

His dealings with the men under him in the guard were also above reproach. He was not highly social, but could think of no enemies made among his friends or neighbors.

After a very short time, it was quite natural that he should reach back through the past and clutch the single episode in his life where he had made real enemies.

This was the army thing, the court-martial of Cal Morgan, Sherman Hambrick, and Barney Sykes. He had a large sense of guilt about the court-martial because no amount of rationalization had yet entirely convinced him that he had been without prejudice.

Regardless, here was real cause for hate and vengeance. And further, the manner of vengeance was in keeping with the mentalities of these men as he knew them. For instance, who else would be aware of his terror of spiders?

In fact, if he didn't know these men were under life sentence at Leavenworth, the whole business would be crystal clear.

But having thought about their hate and his guilt, he went on, as he had many times before, to dredge up the whole dirty business for inspection.

Shortly after Pearl Harbor, he had come out of OCS at Fort Benning, a buck lieutenant. He was sent to Fort

Ord, California, as part of a training cadre for infantry. In six months, he made First Lieutenant and Executive Officer. In less than a year, his CO became battalion commander and he was made Captain over the outfit — B Company.

Secretly he resented his stateside security as a training officer. Thus, while many of his fellow officers were so overjoyed, he was forced to keep his attitude to himself. When he was refused transfer to combat, he turned all of his ardor to the training of troops.

Meanwhile, Madge had been staying at a hotel nearby. Then, because he was on a permanent basis, he was provided with a small cottage and Madge moved to the post.

They were happy during this time, though Driscoll made himself available as a twenty-four-hour soldier and Madge suffered somewhat for the need of more companionship. But Driscoll reminded her that she was lucky to be close at all with so many separated completely.

Madge was sober enough about the war, but she neither understood nor liked the ways of the army with its officer cliques and class barriers against enlisted men and their wives, many of whom she had found companionable during her stay at the hotel. She found the discipline and protocol all a trifle overdone and silly. She was inclined to kid Driscoll about it and to make light of some of his heavier thoughts about the war and the training.

He took it good naturedly enough, explained as to a child and eventually kept most of his military life and its involvement's to himself.

But there was never any lack of real understanding between them. She seemed totally his woman. She gave him love and loyalty. She was intelligent and stimulating. She was full of fun, a perfect foil when he became too grim, too serious in the role he played. She was also superbly gifted in bed and in those days, seldom reluctant with her talent.

He had been slow to marry her or anyone. But having done so, he was deeply, irrevocably in love.

So that when he discovered she was having an affair with a common enlisted man, it was like a blow on the back of the head delivered in the darkness of his own house.

One morning, Driscoll received orders from Regimental HQ to submit a list of names of all troops in his company with battle experience, such troops to fill vacancies in a division soon to embark for a combat area. These men were to be held in readiness but their names were not to be posted until further orders.

Driscoll had no choice but to list the names of Hambrick, Morgan, and Sykes, among others. In fact he was a little relieved to see them go. They had been constant trouble-makers from the time he had been unable to explain to them about the delay in their furloughs, a matter over which he had no control. He had understood their need to go home and he had been more than patient with them, though they were undermining discipline and causing unrest among elements of the company. In the end, Morgan was so often on report from his platoon sergeant that Driscoll reluctantly placed him on permanent KP.

Three weeks later, as part of the training, Driscoll took his company on a disciplined day's march to a bivouac area where they dug foxholes and took up defensive positions for the night. To simulate combat conditions, hot food was not trucked to the field, each man having been provided with K rations.

The following day was to be employed with the

march back.

Just after dark, quite unexpectedly, a jeep arrived from Regiment to pick up Driscoll and return him there for a briefing by the regimental commander. Orders had come through for the assignment of troops to the division moving into combat and company commanders were to receive instructions as to the arrangements.

Leaving his executive officer in charge, Driscoll returned with the jeep.

After the briefing, during which they were told to post the names of troops to be shipped and allow each man a twentyfour-hour pass, Driscoll decided not to return immediately to the bivouac area, but to pay Madge a surprise visit.

He found the cottage in total darkness. Usually Madge left at least one light in the living room. He supposed she was out visiting one of the officers' wives, although she did so rarely.

He didn't have a key with him but there was an extra hidden above the back door. He went around the house and was groping for it when he heard voices. At first, he thought it was a distant radio and then he was sure it wasn't.

The voices were coming from the single bedroom, which was at the rear of the house. The bedroom had two windows — one facing the side and the other just a few steps from the back door. This latter window was part way open and from it came the voices.

One voice was deeply male — and vaguely familiar. The other belonged to Madge.

The shock was as brutal as death and just as difficult to absorb. He continued to grope for the key. It wasn't there. The door was locked.

Cautiously he moved next to the window and stood listening.

Madge: ". . . affects different people different ways, I suppose. You get ravenously hungry, I get sleepy. But I'm not going to sleep for even a minute because I want to talk. Listen, darling, we just can't go on this way. I feel like I'm in an emotional mixmaster. I don't have an excuse in the world. I mean, he's always been so honest and good with me. And I — I feel cheap."

Male voice: "If you really loved me, you couldn't feel cheap."

Madge: "Oh, Cal darling, I *do* love you. Like no one else in the world — passionately, insanely. But that doesn't suddenly make me immune to Greg. We've been close a long time. It's a different kind of love I have for him and every time I look at him, I'm sick with guilt. Really, I'm physically sick."

Driscoll shifted his position, leaned trembling against the wall. The minute she had said *Cal,* he had put the name and the voice together. It was Morgan. Morgan, who had every opportunity because he was on KP and had remained on the company street to help prepare a hot meal for the men when they returned. Yet how would she ever come in contact with him long enough to — He forced his attention back to the conversation.

Madge: ". . . because after all, darling, I'm the one that has so much to lose. You've been away such a long time. You're still keyed up and a little lost and desperate after the fighting. You're lonely. The first woman you meet who gives you love, has you up in a pink cloud. But then after the war is over and you begin to mix with pretty girls and you get back your perspective, you'll drop out of that cloud and you'll wish you had never become involved with me. The whole thing will be sordid to you — degrading."

Cal: "Nonsense! Listen, sweetheart, if you were free

right now, I'd marry you. In fact, if you'll get a divorce from that two-gun boyscout, I'll —"

Madge: "You don't have to talk that way."

Cal: "If you'll leave him, I'll show you how much I love you. We'll be married ten minutes after you get the papers. Of course, I know I can't offer you what he —"

Madge: "Shhhhh. Just hush. You know that's not important. And you know we've got to wait until after the war. I couldn't get a divorce now. And besides, he needs me."

Cal: "Nuts! I don't want you to touch him again. Ever."

Madge: "Would you really want to marry me after the war?"

Cal: "Ten minutes after."

Madge: "Yes, but how about six months?"

Cal: "Six months or six years."

Madge: "I could never last six years. I couldn't ever hold out that long. Make it six months. That should give you time to think."

Cal: "I don't need to think. But if you insist, I'll make it six months. Not a minute longer. You could go to Vegas and rush the divorce through in six weeks."

Madge: "I don't have any grounds but I guess in Nevada I wouldn't need any. Oh, Cal, Cal! I love you so much. Do you really mean it?"

Cal: "Like nothing I ever said before and I . . . ."

His voice broke off. It was as if his mouth was covered by hers. There was silence, interrupted, occasionally by the faint movements of their bodies on the bed.

Driscoll walked away from the house. He came near to a street light. He removed his .45 service automatic from his holster, worked the action back and forward until a bullet was shoved into the chamber. Gun in hand, he went back to the house.

He stood by the back door for a moment and battled down the sickening emotion the had drained away his ability to think. His first coherent thought was — would he get away with it if he climbed through a window and shot Morgan dead? It seemed obvious to him that he would. An officer finds an enlisted man in bed with his wife. In a state of temporary insanity, he commits justifiable homicide. He invokes the unwritten law. Chances were better than fifty-fifty that in a court of ranking officers, most with wives, he would be acquitted. Or he might serve a minimum sentence. But it would work. The odds were with him.

He went around the front to see if a window was open. He found one unlatched and was about to push up against the frame when a second logic came to.

If he killed Morgan, what did he gain? — Revenge? Yes! And after that? Would he forgive Madge?

Never!

Never?

He didn't know. Likely he would have to forgive her because his love for her was too strongly entrenched. To be separated from her for any reason was unthinkable.

So then, if he forgave her, would she forgive him for killing Morgan, a man she apparently thought she loved far more than he? No, she probably wouldn't. She'd never be able to forget the sight of him lying dead as long as she lived. And if she did forgive him, her whole conception of him would change. So much so that the marriage would be worthless.

He needed time. He would have to think about this in great detail, because now the thoughts were racing through his mind, tumbling one on another before he could sort them out.

But this was clear — kill Morgan and that was the

end of his marriage to Madge. And since Cal was on orders for shipment to combat —

He dropped the gun back into the holster and moved off into the darkness. He felt drowned in loneliness. Walking, he began to weep.

After a while, he went down to the Orderly Room, gave the non-com who was Charge of Quarters the assignment list which contained the name of Cal Morgan and told him to be sure it was posted first thing in the morning. Then he ordered a jeep from the motor pool and was driven back to the bivouac area.

He didn't sleep. He spent the entire night in a whirlpool of thought. He kept asking himself how this could have happened? Especially how could it happen without a sign, without the smallest warning? He could not remember an instance when Madge had come close to so much as a flirtation.

He thought he knew her. He thought she was as bound to him as he was to her. How could someone whose every thought was known to you suddenly betray you? It must be some wildness in her, some uncontrollable impulse about which he was unaware.

And what had he done to make it so easy for her to jump into bed with a smooth-talking lying bastard like Morgan? Nothing. Nothing! The bitch. The dirty, whoring bitch!

It went 'round and 'round and got nowhere.

Near dawn he became coolly analytical. No matter what she'd done, he didn't want to lose her. So he wouldn't confront her. Not now. He'd wait until Morgan had gone, until maybe she would realize that Morgan had blown up in her mind out of all proportion to her feeling for him. She would realize that she had been goaded by no more than a sexual impulse into a cheap affair at bed level. Then he would tell her that he knew by the merest accident. Weeping and contrite, she would ask forgiveness. He would forgive her and that would be the end of it. But if he pushed her now, he might lose her permanently.

Having put the whole thing together with clarity, there was nothing else to think about. So he began to picture them writhing against each other in an orgy of disgusting sensualityand on the very bed where he had slept with her the night before. This brought him back to thoughts of killing Morgan, all the while pounding the butt of the .45 into his palm. So that finally he forced his mind to blankness and then to the silly details of the march back.

At dawn there was nothing inside him but a vast ache of emptiness. He roused his officers and began to shout orders as though the camp were surrounded by an enemy.

He stayed away from Madge as much as possible under the pretext that he was deluged with work on a highly secret matter. He was unable to trust himself to play a part for very long. But for short periods, he became a superb actor.

Meanwhile his anger was heightened when she was lavish with affection, hovering over him and worrying about his every comfort. It made him sick. He had a hard time keeping himself from hitting her.

At night he drank too much at the officers club and returned so late that she was sure to be asleep.

He saw Morgan once or twice but turned away because he couldn't stand the sight of him.

He wasn't surprised when, after the notice had been on the bulletin board a short time, Hambrick, as usual the spokesman, came to him in a hardly controlled rage and demanded to know how the army had the gall to send them back to combat at all, let alone without leave.

Driscoll said he didn't write the orders, but there they were. He denied permission to take the matter upstairs. He had told the Colonel he thought theirs was a special case. But the Colonel had asked him rather abruptly if he knew there was a war on. Hambrick sneered at the twenty-four-hour pass Driscoll offered him, but took it anyway.

In the end, he had to threaten charges of insubordination to get Hambrick out of the room. Underneath he was sympathetic. But he was powerless to help and his own problem left little room in his thoughts.

When Morgan, Hambrick and Sykes didn't return from pass, he sensed right away that, instigated by Hambrick, they had deserted. He wanted Morgan on that ship that would load Friday. Because now there was a chance that Madge was going to sneak off and meet him somewhere. He hoped to God at least Morgan would be caught.

And then when Morgan was caught along with the other two, he wasn't entirely relieved because he was in one hell of a situation. He could still rush them to the boat with a reduced charge of AWOL, or he could hold them for a general court-martial that might get them life and put him in danger of a secret and eternal malice from Madge.

However, he was not unprepared. He had anticipated it could happen this way and he had given a lot of thought as to what he would do. He argued with himself that he could not afford to be prejudiced with one man, especially when his decision would effect the other two. He decided that he would do exactly as he would if he knew nothing about Madge and Morgan. He would hold the three for court-martial.

He kept telling himself that Morgan would be in perhaps greater danger if he were sent overseas. He might not even be convicted.

Having decided that he was only fulfilling his duty as a soldier, he then allowed himself to look at the situation from a personal angle. When Madge heard about it, as she certainly would, he would infer that he had no choice but to obey regulations. Especially since, thank God, she didn't know that he had found her out. Further, she would see Morgan in disgrace, a coward *running* from combat. It was possible that he had run from her, too, without so much as a goodbye. That would help. Oh, wouldn't it!

As he sat in the mess hall listening to their arguments for release, trying to keep his ayes from the face of Morgan, it came to Driscoll again that he must erase from his mind his personal animosity against one man and come to terms with the situation as an officer and a soldier. At the same time he must not forget that he was dealing with human beings and that in between the sterile lines of regulations, there should be room for mercy where the unthinking machine of war had created a special hardship.

Once he got Morgan out of his mind, at least temporarily, the whole thing became immensely clear to him. Yet the moment it became clear, he found himself being swayed by Hambrick. If you overlooked the insolence in his manner, Hambrick made one hell of a lot of sense. While the largest percentage of the whole nation were not even in the service, while they complained of meat shortages and gas rationing, while they sat at home in comparative splendor, these men had fought for years like jungle animals in defense of their country. And then because a peculiar circumstance caused them to be needed again in the fight, a well-earned furlough was denied them.

What kind of justice was that?

He had to keep coming back to his original premise. That this situation was not at all what it appeared to be. It was not so simple. It did not merely involve three men and their special right to fair play. Did three soldiers have the right to desert because they were convinced they were unfairly treated? No. Because they were only three among thousands, perhaps millions of soldiers unfairly treated. The very nature of war was unfair.

But most important, what would happen to the discipline of one company, let alone the whole army, if men were allowed to desert and get away with it?

You would have left only a comparative handful of regulars and patriotic die-bards. The army would be a skeleton. A joke. Throw in the towel — let the Japs and the Germans take over. Because any fool knew most men didn't want to fight. They didn't even want to leave home. They were made to do so.

Tortured, yet believing himself to be totally sincere, Driscoll came to his decision.

But Madge found out from a fellow officer's wife that he had a choice in disposing of the desertion charge and her disgust with him lay underneath her every word and action. So that in spite of his knowledge of her affair with Morgan, he had again felt an unreasoning doubt as to his lack of bias in the decision. To the extent that at the trial he became almost as much a witness for the defense as the prosecution in his presentation of both sides of the case.

But too late. And to no avail.

He was certainly not elated at the outcome. He had expected the court would be much less severe. And now Madge would withdraw still further from him.

And she did.

After a year, there was some return of her old self. But she was never quite the same. The spirit had gone out of their marriage. And it was a wound that Driscoll could never heal. For now more than ever, he could not tell her that he knew Morgan had been in her bed. How could he make her believe he hadn't maliciously sent Morgan to prison?

And over the years after the war, there were many times he doubted himself. Wasn't it possible that he had rationalized those men right into prison because of Morgan? Regardless, he came to feel in time that he had acted too harshly.

Sitting there in the booth, waiting for the taxi, he was thinking how he had a home that wasn't really a home and a wife he loved who wasn't really a wife. And if he and Madge were ever going to have any meaning for each other, it was going to have to be done with total honesty.

It might destroy their marriage, but they were both going to have to make confessions. And he was ready.

Chapter Fourteen

Where the *hell* are the babes!" said Barney. "Keeryst! I wish they'd hurry."

It was three hours after Cal walked in with the stolen money.

"Don't burn out your zipper," said Brick with a grin. "They'll be here. Won't they, Cal?"

"They'll show," said Cal. "As sure as money is green."

"We've got the greenest money in town," Barney said. He poured himself a tumbler full of champagne from a magnum that rested on the floor between his feet. "We could build a whole lawn with what we got."

"Watch your goddamn mouth!" said Brick. "Another bottle of that giggle water and you'll be spouting all over the place about the money."

"Oh, crap!" said Barney. "We're alone, ain't we? Shove the funeral and let's live. Let's live, man! It's been a long time."

"Sure, Barney, it's been a long time," said Brick in a softer tone. He was in excellent spirits himself. But you always had to hold a check — rein when the booze was flowing. "Have a ball," he said. "You got it coming. But when the petticoats arrive, keep the lid on about the dough." He chuckled. "You can think of something else to talk about, can't you?"

"Bet your sweet ever-lovin' ass," said Barney with a leer. "When they get here I talk just one language. Kind they parlez-vous in France. But right now I can't keep my mind off those cool green stacks in the closet. God almighty," he said reverently. "A million. A million bucks. I'm a millionaire!"

"Not quite," said Brick. "When we knock it down three ways, you'll be worth three hundred thirty-three thousand, three hundred dollars and thirty-three and a third cents."

"To me, that's as good as a million," said Barney. "I'm rich. You can keep the third of a cent. I'm not gonna quibble. Imagine that bastard socking away a whole million in cash. I never thought it would come to that, did you, Cal?''

"I expected about half that,'' Cal said.

"Amyway, it was the easiest million a man ever earned in his life,'' Barney said. "Yeah, we earned it, I figure. About four hours' work.''

"Four hours and twelve years,'' said Brick.

"I never figured it would be so easy,'' said Barney.

"Don't let me destroy any illusions,'' said Cal. "But it wasn't a cinch and I did a lot of damn dangerous work. I was lucky to get out of there at all.''

Most of the money was safe beneath the floorboard of a closet and a celebration was about to get underway. And any celebration had to include women.

The kitchen table had been carried into the living room. A neatly folded sheet had been spread over it. On top of the sheet rested half a dozen magnums of champagne in iced paper buckets, along with an unmatched assortment of glasses and a great spread of appetizers bought from a delicatessen. At either end of the table were two tall red candles, wax-sealed to chipped saucers. A drinking glass containing three paper roses sat in the center.

Each of the three men were dressed in their best, Brick and especially Cal looking the parts they were about to play, Barney hard-pressed to look like anything but a truck driver bulging uncomfortably in his Sunday attire, fidgeting with his collar and tie.

"What kind of babes are these?'' said Barney to Cal.

"Don't worry,'' Cal answered. "They've got what it takes. For you.''

"What kind of a crack is that!'' shouted Barney, half rising from his chair. "I suppose they ain't good enough!''

"Hold your fire,'' said Cal, raising his hand, palm outward. "I only meant that I — well, I've had my day.''

Barney sank back in his chair with a sly smile. "See what you mean. How was it? Thrill a minute, I'll bet."

"Shut up!"

"Who you tellin' to —"

"Turn it off! Both of you!" said Brick. "We got a million bucks in the kitty and you guys are askin' for trouble. Whatta these cookies look like, Cal?"

"They come in assorted colors, on order. Blonde, brunette, and redhead. I don't guarantee the colors against water or sun. Two tall and one short. They were all built when bricks were cheap. And though they don't have the faces of angels, the devil would be proud. You'd look twice if you saw one of them on the street. How else can you describe this kind?"

"They fit for tonight," said Brick, rubbing his hands. "They fit just fine."

"I'll take the little one," said Barney. "I like something I can bounce on my knee without crushing a bone. You have any trouble making the contact, Cal?"

"Hell, no. Not even in this dull burg. All you need in any town is enough money and a hungry taxi driver and you've got women. Of sorts. Even a taxi driver can run down something good like this for fifty bucks."

"You gave him fifty?" said Brick.

"Twenty-five now and twenty-five on delivery."

"You better watch it, boy. You pass out that kind of money and you'll be remembered."

"Don't worry. I covered. 'We're distillery execs, top brass out of New York, here to inspect a plant.'"

"We'd better hide Barney," said Brick with a chuckle.

"Now listen, god damn it! I —"

"My God," Brick said. "For such a big ape you sure are sensitive, Barney boy. Just a little needle." He turned to Cal. "You say these gals work in a tobacco factory and do this on the side for kicks and bucks."

"That's right. They party with VIPs once in awhile for a hundred apiece. The three of them live together. They're amateurs in the big league, if that makes sense. They like the subtle treatment, appearance of a cozy party, money under the table. They outclass anything I've seen for hire."

"You talked to them?" Brick asked.

"Sure. They like to meet the customer first. They insist. Driver introduced us with all the formality of a social tea."

A dull chime sounded from the kitchen. Cal looked at his watch. "This will be the party," he said. He went to the door as Brick stood up tensely.

Cal pulled aside the spy flap of the door, peered outside and opened. The three girls who came into the room were handsomely dressed, all under twenty-five. They were the kind of girls you might see at a country club dance or a cocktail party for advertising agency executives. Their smiles, however, were of a certain hectic brightness and artificiality, their eyes a little shrewd and watchful.

The two tall girls were brunette and redhead, the short one a blonde. All had, as promised, voluptuous figures. Cal made the introductions, Marian the brunette, Joan the redhead, Alice the blonde. No last names were given or expected.

In the doorway behind the girls stood the taxi driver with an uncertain smile. Cal give him the twenty-five dollars from a roll in his pocket. The driver winked and departed. Cal closed and locked the door.

Like musicians tuning up, the girls moved around the room, getting the feel of it and the men it contained, glancing at the table set up with its champagne and pathetically contrasting candles and flowers, smiling, dropping little feeler remarks and gently probing questions. Finally, each with a brimming glass of champagne, each tacitly chosen by a man who hovered near, they sat down. Brick had taken the redhead, leaving Cal to the brunette and Barney to his blonde.

"Well," Brick said expansively. "This is good. Real good! As you see, this is kind of make-do. We're visiting firemen, so to speak, and we don't have any of the — uh — luxuries of home." He laughed. "Just the champagne. No sterling silver."

Cal observed that Brick was like a man who is fresh from barren Pacific island and has to grope his way in the civilization of women. He was certainly on his conversational behavior. Barney, on the other hand was immediately in his element. To him this was merchandise bought and paid for and he was ready to use it as such.

"You come from New York?" said the redhead who was seated next to Brick on the sofa.

"That's right," called Barney from across the room. "New York, New York, it's a wonderful town!" Brick gave Barney a look. The redhead smiled indulgently, while Barney, seated on the arm of the chair occupied by the blonde, was already beginning to sneak his arm 'round in back of her.

"You fellows are all in the liquor business?" said Marian, the brunette, with a little sweep of her eyes around the room.

"One of the biggest distilleries in the country," said Cal. "The name shall remain secret for the present."

"I understand," said Marian pleasantly. "From the look of it, you specialize in champagne."

"On the contrary," said Cal. "Good, straight Kentucky bourbon and a few blends. Gin, too, of course. We're like the man who owns a Ford agency and keeps a Cadillac hidden in his garage for vacation trips."

"Cadillac and champagne," said the blonde who was pretending not to notice the fall of Barney's arm over her shoulder. "That's very good."

"Not very," said Cal. It appeared to him that the girls were asking rather pointed questions for this kind of a gathering. But he knew it only seemed that way because they had stolen a million dollars. The girls were just making conversation with natural curiosity about men who must have money.

"You are looking," said Barney, burping against the back of his hand, "at two vice-presidents and the sales manager of the biggest distillery in the world."

"I'm duly impressed," said the redhead, Joan.

Brick gave Sykes a long, cool look. Have to stay pretty sober, he thought. Got to watch that Barney. He's going to expand like a blowfish out of water. "Don't mind him," he said. "He's about half a bottle up on us. And now let's talk about anything but business. We'll get our fill of that Monday."

"I thought you girls were Southern," said Barney, gulping his champagne like beer. "I don't hear no accents. Not like I expected."

"Kentucky is kind of borderline Southern," said Marian. "You have to listen real close to catch the drawl."

"Couldn't you toss in a couple of you-alls now and then just for kicks?" asked Barney with a silly grin.

"You ask Alice," said Marian. "She might have a couple."

"I'll do that," said Barney, and used this as an excuse for a whispered conversation with Alice, who looked more resigned than happy.

Two magnums of champagne later, Marian had come to sit on the arm of Cal's chair. He had been talking across to her without attempting to corner her. After snuggling up to him, running a hand through his hair and suggesting that he was a lot of man, she bit down on a corner of her hp and seemed to come to a decision.

"I wonder, Cal," she said. "Do you have a little present for us?"

"Present?" said Cal with dumb innocence. "What kind of present? You want a bottle of our stuff? Our line?" He knew very well what she wanted, and it was a moment he enjoyed more than any other of the evening. This was the first feel of power, to have a great sum of money and to dangle it like meat scraps before the hungry mouths of the whining, obsequiously pleading. This had once been his position, now so beautifully reversed. "I think I can get a bottle of good bourbon for each of you," he said. "Glad to do it."

"No," she said. "Really, I don't mean that —"

"No trouble at all," said Cal. "Don't be embarrassed. I think you kids deserve it. We *want* to do something for you."

Marian's face was suddenly drained of its sugarcoated pretension. The polite, coy little girl of champagne and doilies vanished. "Listen, buster," she said with a tight mouth. "You don't dig me at all. We're on overtime. We're on what they call golden time. We don't play for booze and giggles. We play for the fat envelope. We punched in by the clock. Now pay up. Or we pull down the tents and fold the show." She punctuated the remark by running a thumb back and forth over her fingers in that universal gesture.

That's it, thought Cal. Be cruel. Be hard. Who needs you? We have our crisp green friends in the closet, waiting to obey. "Why, Marian," he said. "I'm shocked. Just shocked! And we were getting to be such good friends. But isn't it delightful that you can buy the best of friends. The very best."

"Come on, kiddo," she said. "Come on."

Cal reached in his pants pocket and produced a startling roll of hundreds, which by agreement, he had taken from the "fund." He held the money with loose casualness and inattention, watching the face of the girl whose eyes had filled with the same' wonder of a teen-ager brushing for the first time with the movie hero of her fan club.

"Now, let's see," he said absently. "What was it? Fifty apiece?"

"A hundred. A hundred!" Marian whispered hoarsely.

Cal felt her leg: "Yes," he said. "It must be made of gold. The girl is a walking icon of gold."

Cal allowed her a smile and counted off three bills. How she must hate this kind of torture. This above all. "Just kidding," he said. "Three hundred is a lot of money and we have to have our fun." He passed her the bills which she counted quickly, folded and tucked in her purse.

Her faced resumed its former attitude of cloying friendliness. "I don't mind a joke," she said. "Even at my expense. If in the end, I get reimbursed. See what I mean?" She smiled broadly.

"I see perfectly," said Cal. "Perfectly. Like Palomar. And now that we've had our little joke —" He paused. The crowning glory of the power of money was to be able to be magnanimous. "And now that we've had our little joke, I'll tell you this. If you treat my boys right, there'll be another — twenty for each of you when this charade is over."

"You're beginning to look good to me," she said. "You're beginning to look like a great guy."

"Oh, I am," said Cal. "You have no idea. I've got

greatness I haven't even shown yet.'' And not to you, honey, he thought. Not to you.

Marian laughed the hearty laugh of the newly rich. And when she had subsided, sought the eye of the other two girls, Joan brushing lips with Brick on the sofa, Alice squeezed in the bear-arms of Barney. And when she finally drew their attention, gave to each a small, tight nod. And that was when the party shifted gears, and for all practical purposes, began to roll.

Chapter Fifteen

On the other side of town, Madge and Greg Driscoll had finished a late dinner. In the living loom Madge was turning the pages of *Life*, while Greg had gone to the den to do a bit of ''homework.''

Madge knew there was no pressing business that Greg had to attend to in the den. She had wanted to be alone and she had driven him there. He had come home late in a taxi, saying that he had a minor accident with the Buick. His clothes looked a mess and he was obviously disturbed about something more than the Buick. He was groping for words to tell her what was on his mind but she had been cool and indifferent. She was too full of herself and the strange, exciting afternoon with

Cal to give him an opening for the kind of intimate conversation she felt he was trying to launch. He was sensitive to her moods and, thank God, never forced an issue until she showed by her manner that she was receptive.

Now he was closed away from her in the den and she could forget him. She sank deeper into the chair and after a moment, put down the magazine, switched off the table lamp, and with a kind of sensual pleasure gave herself back to the afternoon — and Cal.

She reflected that she had been too abrupt with Cal at the last. She had not told him what an agony of need she had for him now, how dull and interminable would be the coming weekend. She had not been able to tell him that he had brought love and excitement to her with such startling suddenness it was hard to realize there had been a twelve-year intermission. She had been too hurried and frightened to say these things.

There had been great danger in his falling asleep. How unlike him to be careless. It was the miracle of the mental alarm that must have awakened him at five. Strange. Yet, how marvelous that they were still undiscovered. And that, twice, without her design, they had been brought together. She remembered the first time and a smile drifted across her face.

*I*t was in the Fall of 1944, Fort Ord, California,, close by Salinas and not far from San Francisco. "B" Company, Infantry troops under the command of Greg, then a captain, were on the rifle range. Every day there was a schedule of some kind — close order drill, rifle practice, calisthenics, combat training or lectures of one kind and another.

But Cal, elected most unlikely to become a twenty-

year man, had been made a permanent KP. This was a
dirty, sweaty job which called for rising at least an hour
before dawn and remaining an hour or more after the
evening mess. But there were advantages. When the
troops went marching out to the field for their silly,
tiresome war games, you stayed behind. And between
breakfast and lunch, lunch and dinner, there were long
periods when you could hit the sack, read, write letters
or generally gold-brick around the area.

On this Tuesday of the rifle range, it was Greg's
birthday. And shortly after the noon mess, Private First
Class Cal Morgan had arrived on officers' row, Captain
Driscoll's cottage, with an immense chocolate cake,
compliments of Mess Sergeant Applegate. It later developed that he had asked to make the delivery. He was in
his dress uniform, tie and all.

Madge had answered his knock, a little surprised
and amused at seeing the sun-baked, ruggedly handsome soldier with the great round cloth-covered cake.

"I'm Private Morgan, Mrs. Driscoll," he had said
with a faint smile. "Cal Morgan. I'm in the kitchen. We
whipped this up for the Captain's birthday. Labor of
love and all that, you know." There was a thin edge of
sarcasm of his voice, a wry twist to his broadening smile.
But the lips that formed the smile stirred something
unusual in. Madge.

"How nice," she said. "How very nice!" She gave it
more emphasis than she meant because she had been
bored with the drab tight quarters, the dreary days with
nothing to do until nightfall. It was as though the soldier
delivered excitement with the cake. "Won't you come in
a minute, Cal," she said.

"Thank you," he said. "And thank you again for
leaving off the private. I despise it." He laughed. "It's
ridiculous. There's nothing private at all about the life

of a private."

She stepped aside as he passed into the tiny living room. He's no ape, she thought: bright personality. A little brash, but polished.. She closed the door and he stood waiting. "I've already guessed that this is a cake," she said, lifting the cloth. "Lovely, too! He'll be so pleased. I'll take it to the kitchen. And do sit down."

When she came back, he was sunk in a chair, cross-legged, smoke jets coming from his nostrils. His eyes appraised her, not as Captain Driscolls wife, but as a woman. His whole approach was without subservience or fear. That, she liked. There was also about him an air of I-know-women confidence and conspiracy. That, she feared. Yet, her excitement was heightened by it. "Would you like a drink?" she asked.

"Yes," he said. "I'd like two."

Then he intended to stay. "One at a time?" she said.

"One drinking, one waiting."

"You soldiers!" she said nervously. "Bourbon?"

"Anything. With anything."

She decided finally on Manhattans since she had a bottle of prepared mix in the refrigerator and there would be no fuss. She brought them back in champagne glasses. She took her drink to a seat across from him.

"Powerful," he said with a luxurious sigh. "How do you make them so fast?"

"These came made up," she said.

He was silent, considering her with a look that told her he was going to cut corners in his conversation. Relaxed in his chair, he seemed focused, intent. "How do you like this army life?" he said. His eyes were way beyond the question. He moved a pawn with one hand but palmed a queen in the other.

"It's mostly waiting — for me," she said. "Waiting always makes me restless."

"And what do you do when you're restless?"

"Nothing."

"No one to talk to?"

"Wives of other officers."

"What could you talk to them about?"

"Nothing. They're a bore."

He nodded. "They wouldn't like you anyway."

"Why not?" She tried to sound annoyed.

"You'd be a threat to them. Too good-looking."

"But they're married."

"You'd still seem a threat."

"Really, now. Shall we change the subject?"

He shrugged, drained his glass. "The Captain, what is he really like? I don't know him. Not the side you do."

"Look," she said. "I'm glad you came with the cake. It was very sweet. But don't you think you're a little impertinent?" He was. And she didn't care. Yet you had to play the game.

"No," he said, and his smile was charming. "There's a difference between impertinence and real interest."

"How could you have real interest?"

"Isn't it enough that I do? If I explained everything it would take forever. There's a war on. There are times during a war when you have to talk like a telegram. And act like a man catching a train."

"How strange you are."

"No. Just honest. What's he like? The Captain?"

She tried to think what he was like in a word. "Dedicated," she said.

"Dedicated to what?"

"Right now, to the army. Before, and probably after, business. He's dedicated to everything. If he drives a nail, he's dedicated."

"How is he in bed?" said Cal. "Is he dedicated

there, too? I suppose he's very precise."

She sat very still, looking at him with her head cocked, as though she were playing the words back to be sure.

Then she stood up. "I think you'd better leave," she said with a coldness she didn't feel. It was too bad because she was enjoying herself. Yet you had to draw a line somewhere. She was always drawing lines and seldom crossing them.

He stood up also. "I'm sorry," he said. "It was such a temptation. Like wanting to giggle in church." He held out his empty glass. "And you promised me seconds."

As she walked over and took the glass, she held his eye, daring him to laugh. He didn't. But when she turned, picking up her own glass and entering the kitchen, she let go of her face muscles, smiling, even snickering as she poured the drinks. It was such fun, this desecration. Greg was so serious and preoccupied lately. And the soldier — what was his name? — Cal! He had said he was sorry and allowed her to save face. He had used bad judgment in the first place but wisdom in the second. He understood women. Oh, completely. He was fearlessly direct without being crude. From now on, there would be no need for fencing. It was like the first affair, after which pretense was ridiculous.

When she came back with the drinks, he was still standing in an attitude of mock pleading. So she gave him half a smile of forgiveness and they both sat down. Immediately his face returned to its former attitude of knowing confidence. "Now it's my turn," she said. "From your standpoint, as a soldier under his command, what is the Captain like?" She was really curious. Had no idea what he would answer.

"He's a leader of men," Cal said.

"Oh, come on now."

"You didn't really want an honest answer, did you?"

"Yes. As a matter of fact, I did."

"You won't pull rank on me like you did before?"

"No."

"The Captain is playing at war with toy guns and toy soldiers. The way a child knocks off his playmates from behind trees because they're the enemy. Only he's a very grave child. Very serious. Like you say, he's dedicated. Doesn't even know he's a child. That makes him dangerous."

"You don't think this war is serious?"

"Oh, yes. Deadly. Though it would be funny if people weren't getting killed, wounded. But it's not for children who take themselves seriously."

"I don't understand."

"People who take themselves seriously demand that others take them seriously, too. The Captain is young and someday he'll laugh at himself. But before he does, he may make heroes or he may make some dead men because he couldn't. That is, if he ever gets into action. Otherwise, he'll be the butt of a few jokes and no one will get hurt."

"I've lost you."

"Dedicated people are rigid. In battle they will expect the impossible of mere human beings. But the Captain is intelligent. He'll grow up after he sees a couple of hundred torn and gutted bodies. If he was a general, it would be a massacre. You see, they usually just hear the distant echo of battle but don't get their boots dirty. They call the plays by phone."

"Your attitude comes from being on the wrong side of the Captain's rank," she said. "He takes his responsibility seriously — but not himself. Underneath he's a very nice guy. I'm sorry you don't like him."

"I didn't say that. He has some good qualities. Shall

we change the subject?''

"For instance?''

"Do you have a radio?''

"Right over there.''

"I haven't danced in a long time.''

He meant that this would lead to physical contact. He wanted to hold her. She turned on the radio, tuning to slow music. They embraced around the room, bending with the music. And when it stopped, he kissed her. It was the most natural thing in the world. And once done, the most consuming. It was the first time she had crossed a line and couldn't return. There was no way back. And when she knew it, she became fluid, melting against him like some fiery, liquid metal flowing into a mold.

But when she did finally break away, he said, "I'm not sorry for that, you know. I knew it was coming. Once, maybe twice in a lifetime, two strangers walk into a room and right away they set up a magnetic field. It doesn't matter if they're married. They're Powerless. No matter what they do they're going to be drawn together.''

She sank onto the sofa and he followed her.

"Doesn't it matter if a woman loves her husband?'' she said. "If she's always been faithful?''

"No. Because until she comes in contact with the magnet, she doesn't know what love is. She's just been kidding herself.''

He kissed her again. "You can't help it any more than I can.''

"I think this time you'd really better go,'' she said, knowing that if he didn't, there wasn't going to be any time to think. The magnet was going to destroy her will.

He stood up and smiled down at her. It was a wonderful smile, very tender. And she liked him because he knew when to stop. She went with him to the door.

"I could love you,'' he said. "And I'll be back.''

And before she could answer, he was gone.

He did come back. The next day. And the next. And every day that Greg was out with the troops.

He grew on her. He overwhelmed her with needing. Until she stopped thinking about what was going to happen to her snug world.

And then one day they were dancing again. And when the music stopped they just stood there and looked at each other. And knew it was going to happen.

She felt into his arms with a sigh. His hands wandered over her and didn't stop but began working with the buttons of her dress, all the time his voice crooning how much he loved her.

And then, "There hasn't been much time for the overture," he said against her lips. "And you must pretend this is the last scene, third act. I'm sorry. I want you to know I would like it to be different. Because I do love you."

"I know," she said. "I believe you. I have to!"

"Then please don't make me ask . . ."

"It's easy to find," she breathed. "There's only one bedroom in the house . . ."

Chapter Sixteen

*T*hat was the way it began, this first betrayal of Greg. And was followed by such a morbid sense of guilt that it developed into a brief but acute physical illness. For two days she could hold nothing in her stomach and was confined to bed with what appeared to Greg Driscoll to be food poisoning. She let it go at that, full knowing that it was her conscience which had sickened.

But when Cal came again one afternoon, the long speech of protest she had prepared died almost at the sight of him. And as the affair continued, it was necessary to rationalize that she had not known what a mistake she made in marrying Greg until she met Cal. But in all decency, she would stand by until the end of the war.

It was a time of plans and confidences. In the end she even told of the big house in Louisville which contained the secret room were Greg was already beginning to amass a fortune in cash. She had told him so much about Greg, and this was told only to illustrate. Even so, Cal was the first one to whom she had ever told the story.

It was also a time of guilt in a period of fantastic ecstasy, fear, and doubt. She tried to analyze how in a few weeks she had secretly undermined what she had thought was a beautiful and complete marriage. The frightening part was that logically it made no sense at all. Greg had given her everything, had been everything to her — everything but the magnet that was Cal Morgan.

And morally she was limping badly. She was an awful cheat, living off Greg and betraying him in his own bed. And for this she had not a single excuse.

Yet in this life which fled so quickly must there always be an excuse for every action labeled by frail human beings — "wrong?" Wrong for others but not for her. What excuse did you need but that you had stopped merely loving and had fallen *in* love? Was life to be a noble self-sacrifice, a nunnery of rejected desires? What excuse did you need but that you had wanted to go here instead of there, to be with this one instead of that one? Selfish! Cruel!

Oh, yes. But underneath the pretty smiles and the posing of goodness and fidelity, weren't we all selfish? And often, without intention, cruel? Weren't the virtuous so because they had not met with that peculiar circumstance which had rocked them from complacency?

It was not an argument that would stand up in open society. It would not hold up in a court of law. But it was honest. And she would have to live by it and believe it.

She wondered now why life had to be so perverse. Why couldn't she have met Cal — before she knew Greg even existed? Then there would be none of these sordid complications. Meeting Greg, marrying him, like most of life, was an accident of circumstances.

She had been living with her parents and a younger sister in Washington, D. C. Her father was a prominent attorney. She had never come close to understanding poverty. She had been sent to finishing school, then college, returning home for a spell of idleness and more luxury.

Her father was devoted to her and an easy mark. But her mother was rigid, dominating, and all too watchful. Madge wanted her freedom and cast about for work that would give it to her.

She found it — a job which would take her around the country with a team enlisting men and women for government civil service overseas.

The recruiters moved here and there, eventually setting up a temporary office in Louisville and trying to enlist the aid of local radio and television stations for free publicity. Madge happened to be assigned to Greg Driscoll's station. Avoiding lesser authority, she went straight to him. She got free time for spots and on-the-air interviews. And, after much hedging around, Greg Driscoll invited her to dinner.

She was terribly impressed with him. He was brilliant, he was mature, he was full of integrity. Also, he was highly successful and obviously moving up.

She found him a little grave, a little long on dignity. But he was far from humorless and she supposed he carried a lot of responsibility. In his quiet, thoughtful way, he was deeply kind and attentive to her. They were together constantly. She knew he was in love with her long before he did.

When she was about to move on with the team, he offered her a job as public relations director. She knew he had created the job to keep her near. Underneath, he was a shy man and cautious. But in time he would marry her.

She resigned and accepted his offer. She was already in love with him. It was not love as she pictured it. This love was warm and tender, rich and companionable. But not explosive. Not full of emotional pyrotechnics.

In a sense this was a disappointment to her. She

had expected that love would be some kind of a rocket she would ride to ecstasy. She had wanted to be in a torment of passion and excitement. She felt there was a force of dormant desire in her still waiting to be used, still needing some unknown catalytic agent to set it off.

But she was in love, whatever the kind. And she supposed the other was some sort of childish longing that never could be fulfilled. She was quite content to settle for this quieter thing.

A year and two months later they were married.

They were completely happy together and in full agreement that it was time she had a child, when the war came for Greg. Sensibly, there could be no children until it was over.

When Cal came along, she found her forgotten instinct had been right. There was another kind of love. There were hidden depths of emotion that could explode and rocket to ecstasy. And Cal was the agent that set the fuse.

She had nothing but sympathy for Greg. And she would pity him — as all who have given much and lost are to be pitied.

She came to pity him not at all. And in very short order.

She had been with Cal the night Greg took the company on that overnight march. It was the first time they had been together most of a night. There had been much talk and understanding. And much love-making.

Before noon of the following day with B Company on the march back, Cal had come to her and told her that his name was posted on the bulletin board for shipment overseas with another division.

He had been frantic with anger and bitterness.

She had cried and had been in despair of losing him forever. There was nothing she could say to Greg to have

him held. And Cal assured her it would be useless anyway because the order had come from the top. He told
her he was going on pass and that it would be too risky
for her to meet him. But he would be in touch with her
— though he didn't know how or when. Because certainly Driscoll would be about until the movement was
completed.

She told Cal that if anything went wrong with their
contact to write to her under another name she gave him,
care of general delivery, Salinas.

Then she waited.

A few days later, on a Saturday, Greg told her that
three of his men had been picked up attempting to
desert. They were in the stockade, awaiting court martial.

The night before, Greg had come home late to bed.
And in the morning when she looked at his face, it had
been so badly battered and bruised, two of his teeth
gone, she had thought he was in an accident. He had
told her then he had been struck by one of the deserters
resisting arrest. She found him a little strange but she
supposed that he was quite naturally upset over the
beating he had taken and she was sympathetic in the
extreme.

Then the thought came to her that one of the deserters might be Cal. She asked casually who the men
were. Greg told her.

For a moment she held her breath. Then she said
the names of the men weren't familiar but she wanted
to know what would happen to them.

Greg said he wasn't sure — but they were cowards
escaping combat and could get life, even death sentences.

Horrified, she asked if, since they were his men,
wasn't he going to do something to help them. He said

he was powerless, the case would be tried at division level in a General court-martial. It was completely out of his hands and he would be no more than a witness.

There was nothing she could say at the time. But Monday she made discreet inquiries from Mrs. Schwartz, the wife of an officer who was in command of C Company, and found out that Greg could once have dropped the whole thing or reduced the charge. The woman knew this because her husband had discussed the situation with her.

Madge was terribly angry and also confused as to why Greg would have any reason to be so cruel. She was positive that he knew nothing about her relationship with Cal. If he had, his reaction would have been immediate. There would have been a horrible scene with simply awful results.

She was so disgusted with Greg and so worried about Cal, she had a difficult time keeping the edge out of her voice when she again made casual reference to the court-martial. She said she had been told by one of the officer's wives that Greg could have dropped the charges and she was curious to know why he hadn't.

Greg asked a little sharply, "Why is it of any interest to you?"

She said, "Because anything you do is of interest, naturally. Especially when people are saying you did something cruel and harsh."

"People? What people?"

"Mrs. Schwartz for one."

"That shows she's an idiot," he said. "She doesn't know anything about army discipline."

"What's discipline got to do with heart, Greg? I want to know why you did it? You could easily have let them off."

"You sound like you're conducting a trial yourself."

"I just want you to tell me why. Because if you haven't any good reason, then I guess I don't know you at all. And never did."

"All right," he said. "All right! If I was a police officer and I caught three men in a crime, would you expect me to let them off? Or would you expect me to do my job and charge them?"

"I'd expect you to do your job. But I'd also expect you to be human and take into consideration the circumstances."

"Now, Madge," he said, "that's nonsense. A woman's logic. Full of emotion but having no relationship to facts. Let's go on with the police officer analogy. A police captain has three men arrested for a crime. He knows the crime was committed, the facts are there. Having arrested them, does he then don a robe and become a judge also? No! He turns the case over to the courts and the men are tried by a jury. The jury decides if the men are guilty or innocent, not the captain.

"The situation is identical. These men will be tried by a military court, not by me. They may go scott free."

"It isn't the same at all," said Madge, her voice rising. "For a short time anyway, you were policeman and judge both. You had a chance to let them go befire charges were even sent to Division Headquarters."

"You seem to know an awful lot about it for someone who has no concern with it."

"I only know what I hear."

"I see. Well, then, you're accusing me because you heard some silly gossip. I'm telling you the facts. I did what I thought right and I don't want to hear any more about it. The court will decide when, how, and if they should be punished."

"Just words, Greg. You were cold-blooded and ruthless. I don't know you, Greg. From now on, I don't know you at all."

And she didn't. She stopped knowing him because she hated him. Admittedly it was because of Cal. Otherwise, it was likely she would have accepted his explanation grudgingly, but with the thought that he knew his own domain and it was not her business to interfere.

But if she hated him then, she loathed him when Cal was sent to prison for life. She stayed with him only because she didn't know what else to do and there was nowhere else to turn.

She got letters from Cal through General Delivery and later from a post box she rented. She wrote back brave words but the undertone of their letters was of Hopelessness.

Finally Cal wrote it would be better if she forgot him and went on with her life as if he had never existed. He said there was nothing in it but torture for both of them and that he was, for her sake, going to stop writing.

She pleaded with him, but his letters did stop.

She gave up looking into the empty box. She gave up writing to space. But she never completely forgot.

Greg was, if anything, more kind and thoughtful of her than ever. Slowly she returned to him. But only part way. She couldn't forget his cruelty and there was always some feeling of her own guilt. But Cal was a secret she was going to keep all her life.

T he war ended in less than a year, before Greg ever was tried in battle. They returned to the house in Louisville and life was much as before. Except that there was always an invisible barrier between her and Greg. She lived in the privacy of her thoughts. And perhaps sensing it, he came more and more to do the same, directing his energy with unusual dedication to the accumulation of dollars, properties, possessions, seldom ever again discussing the secret room.

There was one brief, time of partial closeness. That was during the period shortly before and several months after Bobbie was born. When he was released from service, Greg said there was no reason now why they shouldn't have a child. At first Madge said she had changed her mind. She didn't want to be tied down with children. What she meant, of course, was that she just plain didn't want a child of Greg's. But after a while another thought came to her. Perhaps a child would fill the emptiness in her life over the loss of Cal. And once her love had an outlet, there might even be a little left over for Greg.

It didn't quite work out that way. In the last stages of her pregnancy she began to draw close to Greg. And for months after Bobbie was born, the wall between them thinned. But she soon found her new feeling for Greg had been a thing of circumstance, the sharing of a mutual experience. She loved Bobbie, but now she loved him independently of Greg, as though she alone had created an image of herself.

Again she grew restless and dissatisfied. Her deeply banked resentment of Greg came to the surface. There were lots of subtle ways for revenge. Revenge by making Greg jealous while restlessly in search of a replica or substitute for Cal Morgan.

Sometimes in the distortion that alcohol lends to merely attractive males at cocktail parties, she would think she had found Cal's likeness. At such times it took only the lift of an eyebrow, the most casual flattery or innuendo to have her prospect in hot pursuit. Then, ignoring the coldly jealous eye of Greg, she would follow through with a kind of conversational love-making, sometimes promising a secret meeting. But in the sober light of day, she would see that she had bargained for nothing more than a cheap affair. She then pretended to her disappointed romeo that it had all been a joke and how could he possibly think that she was for one moment serious?

The whole thing gave her a certain cruel pleasure and she never again had to cross the line she drew for herself. That is, until the night of the Florida vacation house party when she met a man who not only looked like Cal, but had the same secret knowledge of women, the same quick smiling confidence and veiled disdain.

She was in an unreasonably foul mood on this night. For a week the lush, tropic atmosphere, the bath-warm ocean canopied with its tiara blaze of stars had disturbed all her old longings for Cal. So, as clouds gather rain for a storm, she had gathered self-pity for rebellion.

While Greg talked his eternal business in the house, she and the man called Mat Tolson had donned bathing suits and sneaked off down the beach for a brief but violent affair. Afterwards, when they were swimming together in the nude, Greg had come along in search of her. They had seen him from the water and had evaded him. Later, he was suspicious. But he never caught on.

The following day when Mat Tolson called her, she told him she never wanted to see him again.

Promiscuity, as such, did not interest her. She was looking for that replica of Cal.

And then only today she was driving down the road and she turned her head and there he was.

She had picked up the magazine again and was managing some small concentration, when Greg came into the room from the den. He dropped into a chair opposite her with a sigh.

"Finished with your business, dear?" she asked.

He smiled. "All through," he said pleasantly. "Getting late." He looked at his watch. His dark eyebrows arched upward slightly. "Going on eleven and we haven't spoken ten words. I don't know anything about your day. I suppose you went to the movies. Otherwise, did anything happen worth telling?"

She put down the magazine and stretched. "No," she said. "Nothing ever happens here. Nothing at all."

Chapter Seventeen

*I*n one of the bedrooms lying next to Alice, Barney was drunk. Not so drunk that he was a physical slob or a mental idiot. But nevertheless, the champagne was gone and about a third of the drainage gurgled in his stomach and vaporized in his brain.

Now that he had scratched a twelve-year sensual itch, the whole complexion of his mood was changing, his view becoming distorted. Lying silently on his back next to the big-breasted, petite blonde, Alice, he felt a vast emptiness consuming him. It was not the emptiness of disgust which might have followed his purely animal release with an expensive prostitute. On the contrary, and to his amazement, he felt something like respect for this girl who had endured him with what seemed to him affection, though it was nothing more than a pitiful resignation. No, this was an emptiness which comes when a lesser need has been fulfilled and a greater rushes in to replace it. The need had been born more than a decade ago when Mary had deserted him and had since, of necessity, been walled from consciousness. But now in this alcoholic haze, there was neither the necessity nor the will to hold it back. And strangely, the girl beside him had lost identity. She was only a girl. His girl. Alice.

His hand crept to hers in the darkness and held it. "Alice?"

"Unh-huh."

"Sleepy?"

"Not much."

"I feel kinda funny, Alice."

'Yeah? How?"

"Don't know. Head feels like a great big god damn floating balloon."

"Too much champagne."

"No! Listen to me, Alice honey. I like you. I really do."

"So? You like me. You like champagne, money, houses, cars and cheese. So do I. So what's it mean, like?"

"It don't mean anything. You wouldn't understand. So shut up."

"Sleep it off. In the morning you'll feel better."

He turned toward her, bent over her. "No!" he said fiercely. "Now listen to me, Alice. Just listen! I love you, Alice. Do you hear that, god damn it! There's your word. Love! Love! I love you."

"You're crazy. And the word is drunk. Drunk!"

"No, now, Alice. Don't say that. Don't say it. The word is love, honey. For you."

"Love, then. Love like in booze."

"Don't say that, Alice. Don't say that again. Or, so

help me, I'll —'' He raised his fist, then let his hand drop limply. ''Help me, Alice. For God's sake, help me! Say you love me, Alice. Say it. Say it!''

Slowly his head sank to her breast. And he began to weep. And Mary, not Alice, held him and comforted him.

And he didn't hear Alice when she murmured, ''It's nothing new. It happens to a lot of them.''

Y ou're a queer one, you know it?'' said Marian, looking up with wide, curious eyes from her position on the sofa, head in Cal's lap.

''You've seen a lot of queer ones in your time, I'll bet.''

''Odd balls, yes. But not your kind of queer. It's too bad. Because we could get along. Even without money.''

''Come now, let's not go overboard, Marian. Anyway, no one gets along without money. Why am I so queer?''

''Because you're just sitting out here talking to me on the sofa when we could be in there.''

''No vacancy,'' said Cal.

''You mean no spirit, don't you?''

''That's right.''

''Some other gal took the spirit?''

Cal considered. ''I suppose that's about it,'' he said.

They fell silent. He was thinking that everything had gone a little sour. He had the money now. The beautiful money. And what else did you need? He should be hard. He should be casual, an unthinking free spender. A playboy. He should make up for the dry, brutal years, the bleak solitude, the crushing loneliness, the poverty of action. He should take this woman like a juicy steak after starvation adrift on an empty sea. The steak would be just as good, though he paid his money for it.

But Cal was worried. He wanted to take his share and run before the trouble started, the real trouble. It would come on Monday when Madge and Driscoll got back from the weekend at Cumberland Lake. That would be when Brick, not satisfied with the money, would want his revenge.

Cal wished he had just driven away with the whole boodle. But he had a certain bent loyalty to the men who had been in prison with him. And anyway, it would be suicide to cross Brick.

But for his part, Cal was through with the whole deal.

Even Madge. Too many years in prison had altered him so that his need for her was a thing of the bed, not of the heart. Really, he must have known this all along, or he would never have used her. And if she ever connected him with the theft of the money, the stars would leave her eyes in a hurry.

"You never intended anything, even before we came, did you?" Marian was saying.

"No. It was for the others. They need it. They need lots of kicks."

"And you don't, I suppose."

"Kicks, yes. But not this kind. Not now, anyway. No hard feelings. Nothing personal."

"Oh, don't mind me," se said. "My meter's running parked at the curb or carrying a passenger."

"That figures," he said. "Keep your flag up, honey, and go right on talking."

W hen Brick saw that the redhead, Joan, was asleep, he got up and began to dress, shoes over bare feet, trousers and shirt. He was quite sober. Unpleasantly so.

His mouth was parched and there was a dull throbbing at his temples. Further, now that this thing was done, this over-rated thing of the bed, this simple gratification which had ballooned in his mind out of all proportion over the years, stoking his anger with its restless need, he felt an unreasonable sense of being cheated. The truth of it was that he had not been relaxed. He could enjoy nothing fully. Because there was much that was unfinished. There was the one great single urge unrelieved. Revenge! This was the real purpose of existence. The rest was so much treading water, a man playing solitaire while he waits for his lover.

In spite of the slight physical irritation of hangover, Brick was experiencing that unusual clarity of mind which sometimes follows after the indulgence of the senses. It occurred to him now that Barney was very drunk. And, though Barney had been warned, boozed up he was full of bravado and he might grow a dangerous mouth. It was only in the heat of desire for the redhead that Brick had been a little careless. Now he despised the weakness that had caused his guard to slip. It might already be too late. He was going to check on Barney. And damn quick about it, too!

Brick tucked in his shirt and tightened his belt. On tip-toe, he left the room, passing into the hall to stand listening at the door behind which Sykes could be heard pleading with the blond.

"What the hell you getting dressed for?" Barney's whisky tenor.

"Told you. Give your boy friend a chance with Marian. They want a little privacy, too. Besides, you need a good snootful of air. You've got love bubbles in your blood. Crazy. What's eating you anyway, sweetie? You go on like this and you'll come apart at the seams."

"Told you, I'm nuts about you, baby."

"About me, no. Nuts, yes."

"I'm comin' with you. Put on my pants."

"Better put on more than your pants."

"Right with you, baby, all the way. You stick with me and you never had it so good."

Silence. Then, with a note of interest, "What could you do for me?"

"Do? Do! My God. My God! Didn't I tell you before? I'm a millionaire. Millionaire! I could set you up like Sheba. And I will. I'll just do that. Remember what I told you. Just remember."

"Come on, sweetie. We'll go for a walk. We'll sober you up. Then if you still mean it. Well, we'll see."

"Sure. I'm ready. Go for a walk. And you'll see. You'll see, God damn it!"

There was movement behind the door and Brick took two quick steps backward as the girl came out, followed by Barney. When the girl had passed, Brick stepped forward and grabbed Barney's arm, pulling him back into the room and closing the door.

"Hey! What's the idea?" said Sykes.

Brick went to the bureau, opened a drawer, came up with one of the stubby .38 revolvers. He held it loosely in his hand.

"What'd you tell her, Barney?" he said ever so softly.

"Alice? Nothin'. Nothin' at all."

"You're lyin', Barney." He pulled back the hammer of the .38, found Barney in one long stride and grabbed him by the hair, pulling his head back and placing the barrel of the gun firmly against his right eye as the lid came down. "Tell me what you told her, Barney. Everything. And I'll know. Because I was listening. I want to hear it from you. Say one word that doesn't fit and I'll have Cal take the girls for a little ride. So they won't hear. See what I mean? I wouldn't need you, Barney. I wouldn't be safe with a liar. And there'd be a two-way split.''

"I'll tell you, Brick. Everything! Every word. Jesus, take away the gun.''

"Come on. Come on. Spill it! Or I'll jam your eye back into your empty head.''

"All right! All right! — I told her — told her I was nuts about her, gonna set her up good. Told her I was a millionaire. Told her we'd go for a walk and talk about it.''

"What else? What else!'' The barrel mouth pressed deeper. Barney's other eye, wide and frightened, bulged weirdly.

"That's all. That's all! I swear to God. I swear on my mother.''

"What did you mean when you said for her to re-member what you told her? Quick, now. Quick!''

Barney squirmed. "That I loved her.''

Brick shoved him away. "Christ! A lousy whore. And you told her you loved her. You're sick, you dumb bas-tard.''

"Drunk, Brick. Drunk.''

Brick uncocked the gun and put it away. He came again to stand over Sykes, clutching his shirt. "You were lucky this time. I know you, Barney. I had twelve years to figure you. You told the truth. But here's for spilling your guts about being a millionaire.'' Brick pulled back is arm and his fist mightily into Barney's stomach. Sykes doubled, moaning, whimpering, as Brick struck him across the side of the face with the back of his hand, and he fell to the floor.

Brick spoke softly. "You're lucky, Barney. You're lucky this time. And so are the three whores. Because if you had spilled it, only two of us would ever have walked out of this apartment. You guess which two, buddy boy. You just guess which two.''

Chapter Eighteen

When Driscoll smashed his car that Thursday afternoon and came home in a taxi, he had been ready to have a serious talk with Madge. He needed to tell her what was happening to him, how worried he was now that he was certain someone was trying to kill him. He wanted to confide this to her and maybe if she was a little sympathetic, to clear up once and for all the thing that lay between them.

But Madge had been especially remote. She had seemed far away, detached. He had decided the time wasn't right and had kept the problem with him in a lonely corner of his mind.

Long after Madge was asleep, he was wide-eyed in the darkness next to her probing for answers. There was not eves room in him for his usual absorption with business. In fact, he had decided that he wouldn't go to the office the next day but would spend all of Friday with Madge. And no matter what her mood, he was going to have that talk with her.

Here he had all this money in the safe below and he

wasn't happy. A million dollars in cash and he was miserable. Somewhere a killer was trying to squeeze him slowly to death, piling trap upon trap to some unimaginable climax.

The whole plan of the secret room to hoard money seemed now, in the face of this threat to kill him and his separateness from Madge, a rather dreary weakness in his character. He was tired of hiding money and hiding himself. So, in the morning, he would take Madge to that room, open the safe and show her, feeling foolish and yet prideful, what was there. That would be the end of still another secret and maybe this would help his cause with her.

It would be necessary to tell her in more detail why he had made this fifteen-year pact with himself. And in preparation he began to sort it all out so it could be explained with some kind of clarity. Though in truth, it was less logical than psychological.

One of his greatest weaknesses was the fear of poverty. He had lived with poverty all of his youth. His father was a second-rate pianist who traveled most of his life with second-rate bands. Or stayed in Louisville to work in sad little back-street joints with pick-up combos. Much of the time, his father didn't work at all. And when he did, most of his money went for booze and later "tea." He died an incurable addict. But long before, he had made it quite clear that Gregory was a mere whim of his mother, tolerated in a weak moment. And further, that Gregory was a nuisance, because, of course, he was a financial drain. Driscoll could never rid himself of this feeling of being unwanted.

There was no help from Driscoll's grandfather, who turned his back when he discovered that his son had no use for what Grandfather Driscoll called work and spent his handouts for anything but bread. There was no help at all until Driscoll's father died.

Meanwhile, they lived in a broken and scabby part of town on the edge of the colored section. The poorest of colored sections. For there were many colored people who lived better. And Driscoll's mother was without any special skills. In the end, she became a checker at a supermarket.

Right or wrong, his mother was full of self-pity. She whined endlessly about the scarcity of money. To her, it was quite naturally the single goal of life, the one importance. She played the tune over and over until it became a one-track recording in the brain of Gregory Driscoll. Distrusting her husband, banks, investments, all public institutions, his mother kept what money they ever had hidden in various secret corners of their crumbling house. Driscoll saw and remembered. He never outgrew his mother's distrust and fear.

When to his amazement, his grandfather left him this great sum of money, he came to a secret conclusion. One day he would build this capital into a million dollars cash. Then he would never again be afraid of poverty. And this cash would not be entrusted to any bank (how well he remembered the wholesale closing of banks) or other institution with the bait of interest. Banks failed. Stocks were wiped out, businesses went bankrupt. No, this great hoard of cash would be deposited year on end in a great safe to be walled away in a secret room of his house, locked and guarded against all but one, the woman he would marry.

This was decided in 1939. In order to discipline himself to the task, have some kind of road map, Driscoll allotted himself a certain number of years to gather the million. To be exact — fifteen. Thus, by 1954, the purpose must have been accomplished. It was from the years thirty-nine to fifty-four that he got his combination 3-9-5-4. The numbers became a kind of superstition. He had them for his safe, the electric door lock and on his license plate. They were engraved on his mind.

The money came slowly at first, but steadily. Then the safe began to grow large amounts of it. Even during the war, it collected for his return, though not in the safe. And in the end, during the last two years, it came so fast he had to divert some of it to business enterprise. Always methodical, he could not allow the million to be early or late. It was to be there in the year 1954. And it was.

He had never told Madge the whole of his reasoning. Never told her the amount in the safe. And though at this moment, looking back, it all seemed a little childish, he was proud of the achievement.

Having formulated his thoughts about the money, he went on to a cooler analysis of what person or persons could be wrecking this revenge on him. By a process of elimination, he always came back to Morgan, Sykes, and Hambrick. He discovered that he had overlooked an obvious possibility concerning them that he was going to run down by the mere process of a simple phone call.

Next morning at breakfast, he told Madge he wasn't going to the office and that he had several urgent matters he wished to discuss with her.

She seemed surprised and somewhat alarmed. At least, he had awakened her full attention.

After breakfast, he took her to the den and closed the door. He had already decided on absolute frankness.

When she was seated across from him, he said, "It's taken a bad shock for me to tell you that I'm in real trouble, Madge. I'm not only worried, I have reason to be frightened. Not just for my safety but yours. Because somebody, somewhere in this city is trying to kill me."

"You must be joking," said Madge.

He smiled indulgently. "Do I look like I'm joking?"

"No, you —"

"I'm not. And the reason I haven't told you more about it is primarily because we're not very close, Madge. And we haven't been for a long time."

"Not close?"

"No. Not close. And it isn't altogether your fault. In fact, it's just as much mine. But we'll clear that up, if we can, after we get to the more immediate business of someone trying to kill me. And, of course, if someone is tryin to kill me, you could get hurt, too, if only by accident."

"Tell me about it from the beginning," said Madge.

"You know the beginning," he said. "That was when the utilities were turned off. It was just the warm-up. The rest has to do with that three a.m. phone call, an attempt to wreck the Buick and poisonous spiders, which indirectly did wreck it."

He told her the whole story.

"My God," she said. "How awful! I had no idea. Oh, Greg, what an ordeal for you. You could have been — Have you called the police? You have friends in the department."

"If I didn't have friends there I might have called long ago. To Gibson or even Kelly, my story would sound ridiculous. There's no real evidence. It all sounds like a bunch of coincidences. They would want names, or at least descriptions. I haven't either."

"I can't think of a soul who would want to harm you, Greg. Have *you* any ideas?"

"Oh, yes. I've had a lot of time to think about it. And there are 'only three' people in the world I know who have both the motive and the knowledge for this scheme. But not the freedom."

"God in heaven, who?" said Madge.

This was the part he dreaded. Because it would

bring back the whole sordid mess. On the other hand, it might be the best way in the world to lead into it and clear it up.

"Three men who are now in Leavenworth prison — Morgan, Hambrick, and Sykes."

He was watching her closely and she looked definitely startled. "You mean," she said, "the ones you sent up for desertion?"

"I *charged* them; but a court martial convicted them." He still found it necessary to defend himself.

"But if they're still in prison —"

"That's the rub," he said. "Maybe they're not."

"I don't understand. They got life."

"True," he said. "That's what kept them out of my mind for any serious consideration. But I overlooked one thing. After the war was over and the hoopla died down, there was a more-or-less general amnesty for prisoners of that sort. Some were released, others had their sentences reduced. So you see, they could be out."

"Yes," she said. "I suppose that's true. And who else would have so much reason to —"

"Would you like to go into that?" he asked.

"No," she laid. "I wouldn't."

"I would," he said. "And right here and now. Because I think you know it's that very situation which has kept us, in some insidious and subtle way, about half a world apart."

He was still watching her ever so closely. She was biting her lip and frowning. Her eyes had slid sideways as though some process of revelation were going on in her mind. It was not the reaction he had expected. She seemed more puzzled than belligerent.

"That was long ago," she said. "And I admit that at the time I thought you were despicable. But I'd forgotten about it."

"No, Madge," he said quietly. "You never forgot about it. There was a reason why you *couldn't* forget it."

Her eyes flicked wide. "And why was that?"

"Because," he said gently. "Cal Morgan was your lover."

She sprang out of her chair. "How dare you!" shy shouted. "Just what do you mean?"

"Now, Madge," he said with kindness. "Please just sit right down again and don't get upset. I've known about it for years and I forgave you long ago."

She sank back into the chair. "How did you find out?" she said wearily.

"By accident," he said. "I was called back from an all-night bivouac for a briefing at headquarters. I think you'll remember. There was a day march to the area. We stayed overnight and marched back. But I returned for a few hours that night and I went up to the cottage to — well — just to say hello."

Then he told her the least humiliating part of what he heard. He didn't want to make an ordeal of it.

"That was just before Cal was caught," she said finally. "And you never told me you knew about us. Instead you had to have a sneaky revenge. So you sent him to prison to get him out of the way. And to do it, you had to send two others. Oh, my God. That's inhuman."

"I don't suppose you'd ever believe me," he said, "if I told you that I tried to clear all thought of revenge from my mind before I came to a decision. I tried to do exactly what I would have done if I had never known about you and Morgan."

"No. I wouldn't believe that," she said.

"The trouble is," he went on, "I've never known whether to believe it myself. It's possible I was influenced subconsciously. I don't know. But the reason I — couldn't tell you I knew about Morgan is obvious. I was afraid you would think just what you're thinking now."

"Do you blame me?" she said.

"No, but I want you to be fair with me. Will you try to be fair?"

"I'll try."

"All right. I didn't railroad those men, did I?"

"What do you mean?"

"I mean I didn't trump up charges. I — didn't frame them. They *were* attempting to desert and they would have missed shipment to hazardous duty. In other words, the charges were perfectly just by the army code."

"I suppose. But you were a low beast to make the charges stick out of revenge."

"All right, if you want to have it that way. It was cruel under the circumstances. I'm not going to deny it. My God, I've felt guilty about it for years. But remember this — if they had gone into combat, they might have been killed. Don't think I wasn't aware of that, though it didn't come into my reasoning. And further, the decision of their sentence was left up to a court martial, not to me."

"You were very helpful, weren't you?"

"I think that's enough," he said. "If you want to go on hating me, I can't stop you, But there are two sides. How about Morgan? How do you think I felt?"

"I know," she said. "It was base. It was cruel. I have no excuse. But I loved him and I was without any will of my own."

"I had to live with that memory all these years," he said.

"But you forgave me?"

"I hard to. I loved you too much to do anything else."

He kept watching her face and it seemed to him that

she was more forgiving of him and contrite than he had ever hoped. It puzzled him.

"How do you feel about Morgan now?" he said.

"I don't know," she said. "I don't know what I feel for him."

The way she said it, he knew it was the truth.

"You really think all three of those men are out of prison?" she asked warily.

"Naturally what you're really wondering is if Morgan is out," he said. "Well, I don't know. But I have the feeling they've all been released. For one thing, they are the only ones who know I have a dread of spiders. Anyway, I'm going to make a call to Leavenworth and find out."

"Do you think," she said nervously, "that — well — for instance, a man like Cal Morgan would be capable of trying to kill you?"

"I'm afraid you'd know more about that than I. In all fairness, he doesn't seem like the type. But it's very possible. The other two are capable of anything. Anyway, I'd like to drop the personal aspects of this thing for good. I have only two more words to say for my part — I'm sorry."

"And, for my part, I'm sorry, too. I don't want to talk about it again."

"All right. Do you think we can ever have what we once had together?"

"I don't know," she said. "I'm much too confused. You're so good, Greg. But at times you're so strange I've wondered if I ever got to understand you."

"You mean about the money? The room?"

"Yes. That's one thing."

"Come with me, Madge." He stood up abruptly. "There are going to be no more secrets."

She followed him to the basement.

He unlocked the door to the workroom and they went in. He reached under the bench and opened the switch, explaining how this cut the alarm to a protective agency which in turn signaled the police. Next he explained the combination for the button that opened the ceiling panel and how this combination worked for the safe with the addition of the number nineteen repeated.

Now he pressed the button repeatedly until the panel opened and the ladder came down. As she had before, Madge watched in amazement.

Now he instructed Madge to mount the ladder simultaneously with him but a rung above. They were carried aloft. The panel closed beneath them.

He stood in front of the safe and for several minutes explained, in more detail than he ever had before, how and why the plan had come about.

"Oh Lord!" she said. "You had a terrible childhood. It's so much easier to understand this when you know the whole story. How — how much did you finally —"

"Ahhh," he said. "I've been saving that for the last. How much money do you think there is in this safe?"

"I can't imagine," she said. "Fifty thousand?"

He laughed.

"A hundred?"

"In some ways, you're a little girl," he said. "I'll call the numbers and the turns while you open it. Then we'll see."

When with his help she had run the combination, he shoved down on the handle and pulled the door open.

The happy expression of one who is about to reveal a mighty secret of which he is justly proud slowly faded from his face. For a long moment, he stared into the empty cavern of the safe. Then he turned.

Their eyes met, a expressions in their faces similar, jaws unhinged, eyes wide with shock. Crouching, Driscoll looked again, as though in the first instance he had suffered an illusion. Then he straightened, rubbing his eyes, leaning on the safe door for support.

"Gone," he said. "Gone. How could it be? My God, how could it be!"

"I — don't know," she said. "Who could possibly —? I mean, it's — it's unbelievable!"

"Stolen," said Driscoll softly. "A fortune. Stolen." He looked like a man who had been struck with a club. "Do you know how much was in that safe?" he said reverently.

Madge was unable to do no more than shake her head. The first hazy picture of Cal Morgan was already forming in her mind.

"A million dollars," he said. "A million dollars!" he shouted. "About ninety per cent of all the cash we have in the world."

"Oh, Greg! I'm so sorry. A million! That's more than I ever — Call the police. Right away!"

Driscoll, leaning on the door, peering into the safe, was silent for something like a minute. He took a deep breath and turned again to Madge. A stony quality had come to his face. "All right," he said. "There's no time for moaning now. The money's gone. But this is clear. You and I were the only ones who knew. You didn't take it. You didn't even know the combination. Now. Who did you tell?"

"Why, I — No one. Of course!"

Staring at Madge, watching every line of her face, Driscoll knew she was lying. "Oh, yes," he said. "You told someone. I can read it on your face. You're frightened. Terrified. Of me." Suddenly he seemed to wilt a little, as though pressed down by too many conflicting emotions. "You made a mistake," he said. "You happened to tell the wrong person. Now, who was it? Are you going to aid a criminal!"

"No."

"Then who was it?"

"I — I don't know where to begin. I'm going to have to tell you how I happened to let it slip. And — and that's so awfully difficult."

"Never mind. Never mind! Just the name. The name!"

"He — It's Cal Morgan."

"Morgan! You mean to tell me that —"

"Yes. He's out."

"And he's been *here?* In this house?"

"Once."

"Oh, my God! Oh, Christ! He comes here to steal my money and to kill me and you have him in the house. You fool!"

"I didn't know, Greg. Honestly, I had no idea!"

"How did he get into this room and open this safe? Can you tell me that? Can you!"

"I don't know exactly. He knew about the room because I told him long ago, that time in the army, and he must have — come down here and —"

"How would he get the combination and turn the alarm off? Obviously, he didn't break in."

"I did mention that you used the same numbers to open the panel from your license plate."

"How brilliant of me to have told you that much," he said. "Then he must have figured it out from there, though God in heaven knows how. How did he have the opportunity?"

"I — I fell asleep. And then he must have —"

"You fell asleep. You were — never mind. Spare me the details. So, while you were asleep, he stole off with the money. Or his pals were waiting outside and they came in and helped him. All right. So what do you think of Morgan now?"

She began to cry and then sobbing, leaned against him. "I despise him," she choked. "Forgive me, Greg. Please, please forgive me."

"You ask a lot," he said. "A million dollars' worth of forgiveness. And you've never been quick to forgive me. If I forgave you, would you be worth a million dollars to me?"

"I'd try to make up for it," she said, against his shoulder. "If there's a million dollars' worth of love, I'd try to give it to *you*."

He didn't want to forgive her. But he knew he was going to sooner or later, and he could feel his fury melting already. Because this would be the end of their separateness, and he so needed her love.

"All right," he said softly. "But will we ever have trust between us again?"

"Yes, if we try hard enough. I love you."

He kissed her gently. "Well," he said, "there's nothing left for us here. Let's go back to the den and see what we can figure out."

"Are you going to call the police?"

"First, tell me where Morgan is staying."

"I don't know. He didn't say."

"Then we have nothing to go on."

"Yes we have. Because he's going to call me Monday to arrange a meeting. He thinks we'll be at Cumberland for the weekend."

"Well, we won't. Not now. And I'll be right here Monday when he calls. Then you'll arrange a meeting with him. But the meeting will be with the police!"

Chapter Nineteen

Cal Morgan looked out the window into the darkness of Monday night and then back at Brick. "I still think you should have let me call her today," he said. "She's going to wonder. She's going to get suspicious."

Brick, who was seated across the room and was spooning beans from a can into his mouth, swallowed, said, "Let her be suspicious. Suppose Driscoll got a peek at that safe just for kicks. Then the wife might figure it out and spill to him because she wouldn't like you any more, lover boy. And then what happens? Driscoll has the phone tapped and maybe by some chance, they trace you down. No good. Better this way."

"Too bad the spiders didn't finish him," said Barney, laying down the newspaper he had been reading. "Then it would have looked like an accident. Here I bring them little bastards in a box all the way from the coast and they let me down. Took good care of 'em, too."

"I wouldn't like that, if he'd killed himself," said Brick.

"Why not?" Barney asked.

"Because I wouldn't have been there to see it."

"I saw him after," said Cal. "He didn't look so hot."

"No good for me," Brick said. "Don't like my fun secondhand."

"You got any other tricks?" said Barney.

"A whole hatful," said Brick. "But I think it's time we really sat on the sonofabitch. We give him too much time and he'll call out the whole goddamn National Guard. We can't let him breathe. But he's going to remember those twelve years. He's going to remember us. And I want to see it. That guy is like a disease in my mind. I keep seeing his ugly pan. Go get the rifle, Barney. And the thirty-eights. The court martial is over. We have decided. Now we must carry out the sentence upon the person of Captain Gregory Driscoll, late of the US Army, soon to be late of the world."

"Listen, Brick," said Cal urgently. "This has been a ball. We've had a lot of fun with the guy. We've scared him half to death, stolen his money and snowed his wife. Isn't that enough? Let's clear out of here before they hang a murder rap on us."

Brick still ignored him. But when Barney brought the rifle and the .38s, he opened the drawer of a table and produced a box of cartridges. Silently he began to load the rifle. This done, he cocked it and held it across his knees with the barrel lifted slightly and pointed at Cal's chest. His finger tightened around the trigger. "Now," he said. "What were you saying, Cal?" He smiled. "You'll have to excuse me. I'm a little preoccupied tonight. You tell me and Barney what you were saying about Driscoll. I didn't quite get it."

Cal looked into the mouth of the rifle as though it were a round, hypnotic eye. He swallowed. "Nothing," he said. "You know what I think of Diiscoll. I was just shooting off my mouth."

Brick lowered and uncocked the rifle. "Let's go then," he said. "Let's go get Driscoll!"

Chapter Twenty

'Stop here!" ordered Brick. "By this clump of trees. From here you can see right into the living room. God damn! Look at that picture window. It's perfect."

"Gonna try a little target practice?" said Barney.

"Shut your mouth!" said Brick. "And pass me that rifle."

Barney, in the back seat, passed the rifle forward. Brick inspected it briefly under the dim light of the dashboard. Now he reached beneath him and took from the floorboards a big pair of wire cutters; passing them to Cal in the driver's seat. "Take these cutters, he said, "and clip that telephone lead where it comes into the house. You got it spotted, haven't you?"

"Sure," said Cal. "I know where it is. But now wait a minute, Brick. You've got us out here and we don't even know the plan. You tell us exactly what you're gonna do. Then if something goes wrong, we're set for it."

"No," said Brick. "It's like the army. They don't tell you the whole deal because if they do you get the jitters. One thing at a time. Go cut those wires. Then come back."

"All right," said Cal. "But when that rifle goes off, you'll have the whole neighborhood down on us."

"Listen to this guy, Barney. He's jumpy as a rabbit

with a hot foot. Use your head, Cal. This is no development. These houses are spread wide apart. One shot. It
sounds like a great big dry branch snapping. Nobody
hears. And if they do, they don't know what it is. They
don't care."

"What about the servants?" said Barney.

"Didn't you say they live in a little cottage way in
the back, Cal?" said Brick.

"That's right," Cal said.

"They wouldn't hear dynamite from here," said
Brick. "Come on, Barney. Out!"

Barney and Brick opened doors and got out, Brick
carrying the rifle, now leaning back in the window.
"Park the car up the street a ways, he said to Cal. "Then
get that wire. We'll wait here in the trees. And, Cal?"

"Yeah?"

"Don't get any ideas." He patted the rifle barrel.
"This baby swings in all directions."

"I'm impressed," said Cal. And meant it. "But
remember. Whatever happens to him, she doesn't get
hurt."

Brick's lips twisted in a crooked grin. "She won't get
hurt. Not unless she gets in the way."

"You better be kidding," said Cal.

"Don't worry," Brick said. "Now, beat it!"

Cal drove off quietly, lights out. Brick and Barney
moved into the trees of a small park from which the
Driscoll house could be clearly seen above. They took
up prone positions behind a tree and waited in the
darkness.

W hen he was nearly a block from the house, Cal
pulled to the curb and parked. He cut the motor, put
the keys in his pocket. He got out, taking the cutters and

quietly closing the door behind him. On sneakered feet, he walked until he was at the edge of the Driscoll property. Clutching the .38 in his side pocket, he moved through a ring of trees and up the gradual ascent of the lawn.

Cal was nervous. He was more than nervous. He was frightened. The time of pleasure had passed. All the excitement and sweetness of revenge had gone out of him. This was the part he had dreaded, had not really expected to come about. And, since it had, he had thought to prevent it. But Brick was on to him. Brick was watchful. Brick never let him out of sight once the final step had been announced. Even now, through the telescopic lens, Brick would be viewing his progress from below. There was no escape.

And yet, there must be a way out! Cal had decided. Driscoll was not going to die. Even if he got away with it, this was one thing Cal wasn't going to be able to live with. Therefore, he must warn Driscoll. And he must do this without giving away his identity or being caught. He must also do this without being seen by Brick. It was a terrible problem. He could think of no way.

Another thing. A bullet was indiscriminate. It could pass through a man and kill a woman, too. Above all, Madge must be kept from harm. Use her, yes. But kill her, No!

Cal reached the edge of the house. He walked on rubber legs of fear. Lights came from lower front windows. Here it was dark enough. But not so dark that Brick could not see his silhouette.

He looked up, following the telephone wire with his eyes to where it terminated below an eave of the house. It had all been marked in his mind. It would be quite simple. There was a rose-covered trellis. All he had to do was climb and cut. And Brick would be watching for the loose end of that wire to fall.

He climbed the trellis to the wire. Grasping one of the wood trellis squares for balance, he clamped the wire and squeezed. It snapped apart, the loose end dangling to the ground. He made his way down.

He had hardly touched earth when the sound came — sharp, distant. Crack! Brick had waited only until he saw the wire part. Then he had fired.

Transfixed with shock, Cal listened. There was what seemed like an endless moment of silence. Then, from far away, Madge's voice screaming, "Greg! Greeeeg!"

Then the silence was absolute.

*F*rom his prone position behind a tree, Brick saw Cal park the Ford and begin his climb to the Driscoll house. Next to him, Barney, also prone, watched in silence.

"It's like the army," Brick muttered. "Like one of those goddamn patrols. Hide behind trees and snipe at the little yellow bastards. Same thing. This one's yellow, too."

"Yeah," said Barney in a hoarse whisper. "Clean through."

"That's the way he's gonna get it," said Brick. "Clean through."

Brick saw Cal approach a corner of the house, look up, hesitate. Brick swung the rifle barrel until he could see the dim shadow of Cal crosshaired in the telescopic sight. "I don't trust that one," he said. "Our boy Morgan has something on his mind. I think it's Driscoll's bitch. Whatever's bothering him is strong. I can smell it from here."

"Yeah," said Barney. "I never did trust him much. He's too slick with dames. I never trust a guy who's slick with dames. You take me, I'm a guy you can trust,

Brick."

"Is that right?" said Brick.

"Sure. I'm your friend, Brick."

"I don't have any friends," said Brick. "Just this rifle and the long green in the closet."

Barney lay in hurt silence.

Now as Cal began to climb the trellis, the rifle moved again to cover the picture window. From this window came a blaze of light. And at that moment, Driscoll was seen behind it for the first time.

He was a very bad target. He moved back and forth, back and forth in long strides, pausing, turning, gesturing. He was angry. Or at lest, greatly disturbed. This was obvious. He came to rest finally, his back to the window. Brick framed the back of his head in the crosshairs and waited. Then suddenly, Driscoll turned and, looking out, remained perfectly motionless.

Quickly Brick swung the rifle in the direction of Cal. He saw the wire fall and swung back. It was a beautiful picture. One he would frame on the back wall of his mind for years to come. Driscoll looked coolly angry, determined, arrogant. The way Brick wanted to remember him.

Now Brick's finger slipped inside the trigger guard and took up slack. But even as he did this, he felt strangely dissatisfied. This was not quite the surging climax to his hate that he had expected. He knew why. Driscoll's face was there clearly in the scope. But it was just a face remembered, impersonal, distant. The face should recognize an enemy, react. There should be the sound of Driscoll's pleading voice. He should show terror, scream agony.

But it was too late. As the thought stole upon Brick, he was already squeezing the trigger. Confused, he was surprised when the rifle whip-cracked against his shoulder and he saw Driscoll jerk back from the window, clutching his head.

Chapter Twenty-One

At ten o'clock on Monday night, Driscoll had no inclination to go to bed and he and Madge were talking in the living room about a plan he was formulating to take her to Europe for a month. Inevitably they returned to the gloomy subject of Morgan, Sykes, and Hambrick. He hadn't been to his office since Thursday, spending most of the time in a very successful return to understanding and closeness with Madge. Several times he had gone to the phone to call Gibson and then changed his mind. Shortly after ten they were discussing the police angle and Madge said:

"Greg, I don't understand why Cal didn't call. But do you realize it might mean those men have already left town with the money? Why don't you phone the police?"

"In the first place, I don't think they've left town," he said. "I'll go so far as to say I'm sure of it. If they had just wanted the money they would have quietly gone about their scheme to get it and then disappeared just as quietly. If your sole purpose is to rob a man, you don't begin by putting him on guard with torture tactics and increasing attempts to kill him.

"No, those men came here with two purposes — to rob and to seek revenge. It's even possible the robbery was a part of the revenge, but a secondary part. The main purpose is that I should suffer for their years in prison, and money alone isn't going to satisfy them. It might satisfy Morgan and even Sykes. But Hambrick, never. There's a man whose very existence was motivated by hate. And that hate must have been boiling and expanding for years. Hambrick is the force. He's the leader. And right now he'll be sitting somewhere working up what he considers a fitting climax for his revenge."

"Isn't that all the more reason why you should call the police?" said Madge.

"No. Because what we want to set up is a trap. I couldn't control Gibson. And if I know him, he'd make a big noise, a great stir. He'd turn this town upside down. He'd have the phone tapped. He'd have the house ringed with cops. Squad cars would be cruising up and down the streets. A smart cookie like Hambrick would see trap written in red neon all over town."

"I'm frightened," said Madge. "I'm frightened for you, darling. Suppose they come here tonight?"

"With you here, I don't think they will," he said.

He got up and left the room, returned in a moment with his .45 automatic in his hand. "If they do come," he said, "I'll be ready." He slipped the gun in his hip pocket and crossed to the picture window, looked out, then turned to Madge who was saying,

"To think I got you into this, walking around your own house with a gun."

"No," he said. "I got myself into it. They were wrong in the first place. But I was an inhuman bastard. In a sense, when I sent them to prison I made criminals out of quite ordinary men. They had been brave in battle, they were tired and discouraged. They were desperate for home. They felt cheated by their own country.''

He turned around and peered into the darkness. Somewhere in the city three men were waiting to kill him. He wished that Madge were out of the way and they were coming now. He was tired. Tired of fear. Tired of hate and treachery, guilt, and shame. The waiting was always the hardest.

It happened so quickly, it was too much for the mind to grasp. There was a distant flash — like the spurt of a blow torch. At almost the same instant there was a searing pain across the side of his head, as though the blow torch had licked above his ear.

He never remembered hearing the sound. He jerked back into the room, clutching his head. His hand dropped and he saw the blood.

He heard Madge screaming his name. Reaching for the .45, he knew what had happened. And he knew he was not going to die.

Not yet.

When Cal Morgan heard Madge scream, he knew that it was too late. Even though he hadn't fired the shot, he was committed. Driscoll was probably dead and there was only one thing he could do — return and escape with Brick and Barney.

This was the end of the thing. Brick was an excellent shot. He wouldn't miss. It was murder and regardless of intent, he was just as guilty as if he had squeezed the trigger himself. It had never in the world occurred to him that Brick would fire until they were all together in the trees. He had thought all along that he would be able to prevent it somehow, that being sent to cut the wire was the one big break. But Driscoll was dead. And now

Cal felt a wave of sickness and revulsion for the whole affair that even his share of the million wasn't going to dissipate. What should never have begun was now certainly over.

He raced down the hill of lawn, crossed the road and entered the trees at the edge of the park. He paused, listening. "Brick?" he called softly. "Brick? It's Cal."

"You blind?" said Brick calmly. "About five feet to your right. You're almost stepping on us."

Cal moved in the direction of the voice, further sickened that Brick should sound as cool as a man who has just knocked a duck from the sky.

Looking down, he saw Brick and Barney prone at his feet, Brie still holding the rifle at the ready. "You sonofabitch," Cal murmured. "I didn't thinly you'd do it. I never thought you'd really do it."

As soon as Brick had seen Driscoll's hand go up to his head, he knew that he had not killed him. A man with a bullet through his brain doesn't reach to see what hit him. His brain has no message for him at all. Not even that he's dead. He sinks from life like a stone in water or collapses like a balloon deflating, his only reaction involuntary, muscular.

Brick was not disappointed. In fact, he was overjoyed. Now he would be able to stand a few feet from Driscoll and watch him die. He had been confused in his emotions and this had caused his aim to be a fraction off. His luck was running high. It was perfect. Driscoll would know now. He would lice in terror and pain until the end.

"Just winged him," Brick said to Barney. "Now the real fun begins."

"What — what do you mean?" said Barney with an

awed tone.

"I mean that was just a teaser," said Brick. "Now we'll move in on the bastard and finish him. We'll nail him to the cross and watch him bleed. Then I'm gonna be hungry. It'll be like after a woman. I'm gonna want a steak thick as a baseball bat."

Just then Cal approached, stood strangely still. Brick looked up at him. "You sonofabitch," Cal murmured. "I didn't think you'd do it. I never thought you'd really do it."

Brick felt the slow burn of anger. He swung the rifle so it covered Cal's belly. "Watch your goddamn mouth," he said. "I've got the feeling tonight. Like I've got to see little men fall. You may be one of them, little man." He patted the rifle. "My friend here has no preferences."

"Go ahead," said Cal. "I didn't think Driscoll would be enough for you. Try me now. And then Barney."

"Soft," said Brick. "I knew you'd go soft when the chips were down. You've been tryin' to squirm out of the payoff from the first."

"He's not dead," said Barney. "Driscoll's not dead. That one just burned his head a little."

Brick stood up. He kept the gun on Cal. "All right, Morgan," he said. "After you. Move on up to the house. And, Morgan. You can pass over that .38. You won't be needing it."

W hen Barney heard the shot, he jumped with surprise. And when he saw that Driscoll was hit, the excitement drained out of him. He was like a man who has come with thrilling expectancy to see the result of a devastating accident, and then, arriving on the scene, is too shocked at the sight of blood for any morbid satisfaction.

Up until now, it had all seemed like a big game. Scaring Driscoll was fun. Taking his money was marvelous revenge. But actually killing him was a step beyond the limit of is imagination. He wanted Driscoll to die. But it should be like a movie. You watch it, the villain falls, you feel sated, and you go home without the slightest involvement. You had the pleasure without the consequences.

Brick was too coolly, methodically the killer for Sykes. Yet now it was done and Barney wanted to be gone with his share, gone forever from the unpredictable, dangerous presence of Brick. Then when he saw that Driscoll was not dead, some of Barney's bravado returned. The whole thing became a game again. But now as Morgan led the way to the house under the gun of Brick, a new thought came to Sykes. He drew close to Brick and whispered, "What about the bitch? She's there. She'll remember us."

"Don't worry," said Brick out of the corner of his mouth. "If she's there, she's gonna lose her memory just like Driscoll."

Barney was silent. But this was something else again. Driscoll maybe. But not the woman. He wouldn't be able to stand that. Now he was really frightened. But most of all, of Brick.

Chapter Twenty-Two

*H*olding a handkerchief to the side of his head, Driscoll moved well back from the window. Madge had stopped screaming his name and came toward him in a trance of shock.

"I'm all right," he said. "I'm all right. Flesh wound. Tie this handkerchief around my head. Quick!" He grabbed her arm and took her into the hall out of range.

"Oh, God! Madge said. "What happened? What happened!" Her hands trembled with the knot.

"Rifle shot," Driscoll said. "They've come. No time for talk. They'll be breaking in here next. Got to phone the police."

Driscoll picked up the receiver and dialed. He was too excited to wait for a tone. Now he listened. He dialed again. He jiggled the receiver. "This phone is dead," he said.

"Dead?" said Madge. "It can't be. Try the one in the den."

Driscoll went away and returned. "Dead," he said. "It's either out of order or the wire has been cut."

"You mean to say that —"

"Yes. Yes! Cut. I've got to do something. Something!" He threw his arms in the air. "But what?"

"I'll run next door," said Madge.

"You'll do nothing," he said. "Nothing. Stay right

where you are. Just let me think."

It would be suicide to leave. And just as dangerous to stay. Yet, if they were going to kill him, what about Madge? They wouldn't want her to be able to identify them. In that case — Oh, God!

"Now listen to me carefully," he said. "And don't ask questions." He didn't want to tell her that she was in as much danger as he was, but he had to get her out of the house. "Go out the back door. Turn left and run to the Gresham's place. Don't go below. Stay up on the hill and cross over. Run! Call the police, but don't come back. Stay there! Don't worry about me. I've got the forty-five and I'll hold them off until help comes. II'll go down cellar and trip off the bulgar alarm. It's a separate wire. Now, come on!"

"But what if —"

"Never mind. Never mind! Do as you're told! Back door. Let's go!"

Driscoll peered through the window of the back door, saw nothing. Holding the .45 cocked and ready, he opened the door and looked out cautiously. The night was soundless, he could see no form or shadow in the darkness. He stepped back in and pushed Madge through the doorway.

At that moment, the figure of a man raced from concealment around a corner of the house and grabbed her so quickly, Driscoll was unable to fire. Now the figure, using her as a shield, shoved her back into the doorway. The figure became Sherman Hambrick holding a .38 revolver to Madge's head. Even in the dim light, Driscoll had recognized the tall man. Now there was Hambrick's voice, vaguely familiar.

"Toss the pistol out here, Driscoll! You've got five seconds before she gets it."

Driscoll was in a panic of indecision. Hambrick

might be bluffing. Even so, there was no way to get at him while he held Madge. Bluffing or not, there was little hope but to stall for time. He let the hammer down and threw the automatic to Hambrick's feet. Hambrick recovered it quickly and came forward behind Madge, entering the house and closing the door behind him. "All right," he said, "Both of you. Move! Into the living room."

When they came to the center of the room, Driscoll halted, waiting with Madge. He tried to appear relaxed but his muscles coiled to spring as he turned toward Hambrick. Now was the time, while Hambrick was still alone. But Hambrick stood ten feet removed from him with a steady gun. It was an impossible gamble.

"Well, if it isn't the brave Captain," said Hambrick. "And in mufti. All nice and pretty and clean in his fine big house with his fine big woman. You look old, Driscoll. Old and soft. Well, you're gonna get softer, Driscoll. But never any older. Now, go open that front door. On the double. March!"

Driscoll moved to obey without a word. This was a new Hambrick — a gaunt, bitter-faced man with kill-crazy eyes. Humor him and delay. But for how long? In the face of Hambrick, Driscoll could read only one end to this night.

He opened the door.

He recognized Cal Morgan, his wife's lover. Strangely, Morgan was unarmed. But behind him was Barney Sykes, and Sykes carried a rifle. Did Driscoll imagine it, or was the rifle trained casually at Morgan's back?

Morgan looked at him impassively as he entered the room. Barney closed the door, leered disdainfully, worked his mouth as though over a wad of gum and spat in Driscoll's face.

Driscoll wiped the loathsome drool from his cheek, stumbled as Barney shoved him forward and pushed him into a chair.

Hambrick motioned Madge to a chair opposite. "Sit right there, honey," he said. "Quiet as church. We'll get to you later."

Driscoll decided that it was all over unless there was some way to satisfy the hate in Hambrick without a killing. "Hambrick," he pleaded in a soft voice. "You've got the money. What else do you want?"

Hambrick shoved the .45 in his hip pocket and held the .38 loosely in the direction of Driscoll. "I want you," he said. "All of you, Driscoll."

"It was a long time ago," said Driscoll softly. "It should be forgotten now."

"By you, yes, you sonofabitch," said Hambrick. He looked around the room. "Set up like this for twelve years, you'd forget easy." He put one muddy foot up on the arm of the chair in which Madge sat, smearing the fabric. "But, you see, Driscoll, we had a little reminder. All this time we kept looking out at the world through bars. And there was nothing to see — or remember. But your crumby puss. The little dictator — take these men away and lock them up, Sergeant." He spat on the rug. "You bastard," he whispered. "You sweet-smelling, dirty, arrogant bastard."

Let him talk, thought Driscoll. Let him curse and condemn. It might be the only way. "All right," he said. "You've had a rough time. And you're wrong if you think I haven't thought about it. I was full of patriotism and false pride of the army. I was too bigoted to be human. I made a bad decision. For what it's worth, I'm sorry. And I want you men to forgive me."

"Listen to the bastard," said Barney Sykes. "Just listen to him! Listen to him crawl. Forgive, he says.

Huh!"

"You're late," said Hambrick. "Twelve years too late."

"So now you come back for revenge. What can it get you but more years behind bars? My God, what else do you want? You've taken practically everything I own."

"No we haven't," said Hambrick. "What's the most valuable thing you or anyone can own in this world?"

"I don't know," said Driscoll. He knew perfectly well. But he dared not say it or think it.

"You know, all right," said Hambrick, leaning forward, motionless now, waiting. "But I'll tell you anyway," he finished: "It's your life."

"And that's what you want?" said Driscoll with an immense effort to keep the tremble out of his voice.

"Yes," said Hambrick. "And what we want, we take." Very slowly, Hambrick pulled back the hammer of his revolver.

"Stop it. Stop it!" shouted Madge. "I don't know you two, but I know Cal Morgan." She looked at Morgan in desperation. "He may be a lot of things, but I don't think he's a killer. I don't think he's going to stand by and let you kill my husband. Are you, Cal?" As she looked up at Morgan, a tear coursed down her face.

Hambrick turned to Morgan with a sly grin. "Well, now," he said. "Maybe the lady's right. Maybe Morgan isn't going to stand by and let me kill his friend Driscoll. After all, they're blood brothers. Sure. In a way, you might say they're related. Isn't that right, Barney?"

"That's right," said Barney, pulling the rifle up a little tighter on Morgan's back.

"Well, Morgan?" said Hambrick. He watched the other's face intently.

Morgan's features showed nothing. His eyes slid to Madge and back to Hambrick. He shifted slightly in place. "I think we should give him a break," he said. "After all, it's not an equal revenge. He didn't just take us out and shoot us. We had a trial."

Hambrick made a show of taking this under consideration. His eyes drifted upward in Nought. "All right," he said. "Morgan is right. Driscoll should have a trial. We'll hold it right now. We're a court of three." He turned to Barney. "Barney Sykes," he said. "As a judge of this court martial, have you heard all the evidence against the prisoner, Gregory Driscoll?"

Barney wet his lips. "I have," he said solemnly.

"And, Cal Morgan, have you likewise heard the evidence against the prisoner?"

"Don't be ridiculous," said Morgan.

Hambrick looked at Barney who then shoved the barrel of the rifle in Morgan's back.

"I want an answer, Morgan," said Hambrick.

Morgan sighed. "I'm familiar with the evidence," he said. "Our side of it."

"And I, Sherman Hambrick, have also considered the evidence against the defendant. The court will vote. Guilty or not guilty? Sykes?"

Sykes, his face drawn and shaded somehow with fear, allowed his gaze to rest for a second on Driscoll. His eyes wavered and came back to Hambrick. Again he moistened his lips. "I — guilty," he said hoarsely.

"Morgan?"

"He's had enough," said Morgan. "Let him go."

"In this court, a majority rules," said Hambrick. "My verdict is — guilty! And it is now my duty to pass sentence — unless the defendant has something to say."

"There's nothing I could say to men like you," answered Driscoll. "I ask one thing."

"Well?" said Hambrick.

"That you let my wife go unharmed, whatever you

do to me."

"You know," said Hambrick, "That's one request I'd like to grant." He looked Madge up and down. He shook his head. "Too bad, honey. What a waste of talent. But we can't have her as a witness, now, can we, Driscoll? Tell you what. We'll see that she goes quickly. Fair enough?"

Morgan stepped forward a pace. "Now, listen, Hambrick. God damn it, you listen! You touch her and I'll kill you. I mean that."

"If he moves another step, Barney, pull the trigger. Now, Driscoll, the court is ready to pass sentence upon you."

The fear that was consuming Driscoll left him, washed away by the angry need to protect Madge. He grasped the arms of the chair and waited for the moment.

"Gregory Driscoll, it is the decision of this court that you be executed on the spot, twelve bullets to enter your body, one for each year of your offense, none of these bullets to be fatal — except the last."

Hambrick removed the .45 from his pocket and, holding it in his left hand, leveled the .38 in the area of Driscoll's upper right arm.

Looking into the barrel, Driscoll tensed for his move. At that moment, out of the corner of his eyes, he saw Morgan jab a fist over his shoulder into Barney's face, diving low and forward in almost the same motion, to sweep Hambrick off his feet. As Driscoll sprang from the chair, the gun in Hambrick's hand cracked uselessly.

Driscoll leaped around the writhing men and ran at Barney just as he was coming up from the floor with the rifle, his nose streaming blood.

Still in stride, Driscoll drew back his foot and kicked Sykes in the face as though he were launching a football.

Sykes moaned, fell backward, lay still. Driscoll grabbed the rifle. Morgan had been no real match for Hambrick. As Driscoll watched, Hambrick crouched over him and rammed a fist so hard into his face that Morgan's head bounced back off the floor and he lay still. Quickly, Hambrick reached left and found the .45 where it had fallen to the floor. He jammed the barrel against Morgan's teeth and pulled back the hammer.

Across the room, Driscoll had already leveled and cocked the rifle. When he saw Hambrick reach for the pistol, he shouted a command which, if Hambrick heard, he ignored. Then when Driscoll saw the hammer being pulled back, the .45 at Morgan's mouth, he fired.

For a moment, Hambrick seemed to freeze in position. There his body shivered somewhat in the exaggerated manner of a horse whose flank is stung by a fly. At the same moment, a thin geyser of blood issued from the side of his head, he topped sidewards, jerked once and lay still.

Driscoll watched with mixed horror and relief, finally forcing himself to approach, pick up the .45 and find the .38. Then, covering Barney, Driscoll relieved him of two more revolvers and backed to where Madge sat sobbing in her chair.

"Try to be calm now," said Driscoll. "There are still things to do." He reached in his pocket and handed her a key to the storeroom. "Go down to the cellar and press that door-release button under the table. The burglar alarm switch is closed and it will flash a warning to the police in town. It takes them about ten minutes to come way out here."

Scrupulously avoiding the sight of Hambrick, Madge fled from the room.

Driscoll fell into a chair and laying the rifle across his lap, covered Barney, now getting dazedly to his feet, with the .45. "All right, Sykes," he said. "Step right over there to Morgan and get him up. And, Sykes. While you're at it, take a good look at Hambrick."

Sykes stumbled across the room and stood for several seconds looking at the body of Hambrick soaking the floor. He shuddered.

"It could happen to you," said Driscoll wearily. "Now, help Morgan up."

Sykes, his face raw and bleeding, pulled Morgan from under the legs of Hambrick. Morgan opened his eyes and stumbled to his feet.

"Both of you, sit across from me on that couch," said Driscoll. They obeyed. Madge came back into the room. She sat on the arm of Driscoll's chair. "I pressed the button," she said.

"Brick's dead," said Barney reverently to Morgan.

Morgan looked over at the body but only nodded.

"He wouldn't be dead," said Driscoll, "but he was such a good friend of yours, Morgan, he was about to blow your head off with this .45. I had to stop him."

"Thanks," said Morgan. "He had it coming. He was a killer gone crazy. He might have killed us all. What are you going to do with us now, Driscoll?"

"The police will be here in about ten minutes, sooner if they can radio a car in this area."

"I see," said Morgan. "We should be good for another twelve years, maybe twenty."

"Maybe," said Driscoll. "Where's the money?"

"Don't tell him," said Barney.

"I couldn't care less," said Morgan. "It's under the floor, back bedroom closet. Apartment on the south side — 2370 Middlesex, Apartment 3C."

Driscoll reached in his pocket with his free hand and produced a notebook and pen, passed them to Madge. "Write that down — 2370 Middlesex, Apartment 3C." Madge obeyed. "Let's have the key," said Driscoll.

Morgan found it and tossed it over.

"You wouldn't lie to me about this, Morgan?"

"Why should I? You can check it when the police get here."

"How much of the money is there?"

"All but a few hundred bucks. Just about the whole million."

"I believe you," said Driscoll. It was obvious to him that Morgan was finished with the whole business, had no reason to lie. He looked at his watch. "About six more minutes," he said. "Did you come in a car?"

"Yes," said Morgan.

"Do you think," said Driscoll, "you can take Sykes and get on the road out of town before the police come?"

"Hell, yes!" said Morgan. "You a mean you're going to let us go?"

"I have every reason not to," said Driscoll. "I have every reason to despise you in particular, Morgan. But on the other hand, I consider that you saved our lives tonight and I don't think you wanted any part of this but the money. I suppose I'm partly to blame that you came here in the first place. This will cancel it out."

"My God! said Morgan. "I could almost get to like you, Driscoll. Come on, Barney. Before he changes his mind." Morgan stood up as did Barney. Morgan looked over at the body of Hambrick. "How do you explain that?" he said.

"As far as the police are concerned, he was alone and planned the whole thing. I shot him in defense of my home. There'll be no trouble about it. Now beat it!"

Barney turned at the door and looked back. "Thanks," he said, and went out. As Morgan was about to follow, Driscoll said, "I wouldn't try to go back for the money, Morgan. There'll be a squad car at that address minutes after you leave."

"Don't worry," said Morgan. "We'll be across the border while you're still counting it." The door slammed. He was gone. Driscoll could hear them running. Then, in a moment, the angry whine of a car being gunned.

They sat for nearly a minute in silence. "Don't you think it was dangerous to let them go?" Madge said then.

"No," said Driscoll. "Foolish, maybe, but not dangerous. Those are two men you'll never see again."

"I'm glad of that," said Madge. "I wouldn't ever want to see them again. Either of them. And I don't think you were foolish. Just human."

Driscoll let his arm fall around her shoulder and again they were silent until Madge said, "Listen!"

He did. There was the distant wail of a siren, then another before the sound of the first died. He nodded. "They're coming now," he said. He looked over at Hambrick distastefully. "There was a lot of evil in that one," he said. "And a lot of power. All destroyed in an instant. Makes you kind of humble."

"Don't even talk about him," she said. "I could be terribly sick. What about the money? Those two still know where you'll keep it."

Driscoll almost smiled. "Oh no they don't." He stood up as sirens growled and faded in front of the house. "Hereafter, if anyone wants our money, they'll have to go hold up the banks."

Quite calmly, he went to open the door for the police.